SUBMITTING TO THE DOCTOR

Cowboy Doms - Book Seven

BJ WANE

Published by Blushing Books
An Imprint of
ABCD Graphics and Design, Inc.
A Virginia Corporation
977 Seminole Trail #233
Charlottesville, VA 22901

©2020
All rights reserved.

No part of the book may be reproduced or transmitted in any form or by any means, electronic or mechanical, including photocopying, recording, or by any information storage and retrieval system, without permission in writing from the publisher. The trademark Blushing Books is pending in the US Patent and Trademark Office.

BJ Wane
Submitting to the Doctor

EBook ISBN: 978-1-64563-207-8
Print ISBN: 978-1-64563-255-9
v1

Cover Art by ABCD Graphics & Design
This book contains fantasy themes appropriate for mature readers only. Nothing in this book should be interpreted as Blushing Books' or the author's advocating any non-consensual sexual activity.

Prologue

Denver, Colorado

Soft, white snowflakes fell from the gray sky onto the dark clothing of the mourners slowly dispersing from the gravesite. Doctor Mitchell Hoffstetter gazed with grief-stricken, unseeing eyes at the flower-covered coffin. He thought he'd been prepared for his beloved wife's passing after the chemotherapy treatments had failed to wipe out her cancer these past six months. Last week, he'd stood by Abbie's hospice bed and watched her shudder through her last, painful breath, the peace that settled over her stricken face almost beautiful to see after months of ravaging torment. Following her diagnosis, he'd reached out to the top oncologists in the state for help, cut back on his job as chief trauma surgeon at Denver Health and prayed for a miracle.

All to no avail.

The murmured condolences and sympathetic eyes of friends and colleagues went unheard and unseen as Mitchell shivered against the bleak future now lying ahead of him. He would turn forty-one this summer and yet, instead of hitting his prime looking forward to the future, he now dreaded the months and years that stretched out ahead of him without his cherished wife. For eight years, she had been the perfect wife and submissive of his dreams, the only woman he'd ever vowed fidelity to or imagined sharing his life for the long haul. Her death shattered the dream and left a nightmare he was desperate to escape from.

"Mitchell, let's go. People will be stopping by the house." His mother, Louise, gripped his arm and looked up at him with worry etched on her lined face.

Patting her hand, he nodded and turned to take his sister's elbow. "I'm ready. Let's get you and Tracy out of the cold." He feared there would be no escaping the cold for him for a long time, if ever.

Eighteen months later

The July sun beat down on Mitchell's shoulders as he loaded the last of his suitcases in his Tahoe and closed the back hatch. The For-Sale sign in the front yard of the two-story home he'd shared with Abbie was now topped with a Sold sign. His chest constricted as he took one last look at the flower beds she'd planted and tended with such meticulous care. He recalled the way she would kneel and wiggle her ass, sending him a taunting grin over her shoulder when he would pull into the driveway. The tall hedges in front of the porch offered enough privacy for him to shock her one time and deliver the bare butt spanking she'd been itching for right then and there. She'd loved the exhibitionism and risk as much as the pain-induced pleasure he'd heaped upon her soft, lily-white buttocks.

Sliding behind the wheel, he pulled away for the last time, praying the move to Montana and the new, much less strenuous position of family physician in the smaller town of Willow Springs would offer the change he needed to cope better with his loss. His mother and sister, as well as Tracy's husband and two boys, all encouraged him to accept the position when he found the ad and showed it to them. With his father gone these past five years, he'd hesitated to move away from his mother, but she'd been the one to insist the loudest for him to make the change.

"It's a one-day drive," Louise had said at Sunday dinner last month. "Just be sure to get a place big enough to put all of us up for a week and we'll be on your doorstep more than you'll want."

Mitchell hadn't prayed much since burying Abbie and his happiness, but as he drove away from the home they had shared, the position he'd worked hard to attain and the city he'd lived in his whole life, he found himself sending up a silent entreaty he wasn't making a big mistake.

Chapter 1

Tears blinded Lillian Gillespie's vision as she stumbled out the door of the special care facility. The cold slap of February wind that hit her added to the chill that had invaded her body as she'd watched her cherished twin sister take her last breath. The nursing staff who had cared for Liana for the last month as she lay in a coma meant well with their embraces and whispered condolences of 'it's for the best', but right now, Lillian couldn't see it that way.

She let the tears fall as she slid behind the wheel of her car, slammed the door and huddled in misery, wondering what she would do without Liana in her life. They'd shared the special bond of twins for thirty-four years, stood side by side when they'd buried first their father and then their mother a scant year later, and they'd watched men come and go without regret as long as they had each other.

And now Lillian was alone.

Rubbing her forehead, she tried to gather her thoughts and run through what needed to be done. Once Liana had stabilized following a ruptured brain aneurysm six weeks ago and was moved from the hospital to the long-term care facility with a poor prognosis of ever recovering or even coming out of the coma, the staff had convinced Lillian to make funeral arrangements. At first, she'd fought the very idea, clinging to the small thread of hope the trickle of blood still reaching her sister's brain offered, but now she was glad the hospital counselor had talked her into it. It was one less burden to weigh her down now.

Pulling out of the lot, she automatically drove toward Brad's house, her thinking still muddled by heartbreak. She was halfway to his upscale neighborhood in Salt Lake City when the change in her circumstances hit her with a quick flash of clarity. *I'm free of that son-of-a-bitch.* That startling acknowledgement forced her to pull into a strip mall lot as a cold, burning anger replaced her emotional numbness, giving her the inner shakes. *I'm free, but God, sis, I never wanted to get away from him at your expense.* No, she couldn't look at it that way. It was Lillian's fault for ignoring the warning signs of the renowned neurosurgeon's possessiveness for too long before breaking off their affair. Maybe, if she hadn't been so immersed in her art, preparing for the Naples National Art Show, she would have ended the relationship much sooner. Liana had often berated her for losing focus of everything and everyone around her when she lost herself in her painting, and Lillian had finally paid the price for her artistic absorption.

But no more. Liana's death rendered Dr. Brad McCabe's threats useless and severed the hold he had over her. As much as her passing pained Lillian, she couldn't prevent a ripple of relief as she got back on the road. To say Brad had taken their split badly was an understatement, but she could never have imagined just how obsessed he'd become with her until Liana was sent to the long-term care facility.

Lillian gritted her teeth as she turned onto the street of million-dollar homes and pulled into the drive of Brad's two-story, one-acre estate. No one would ever believe the skilled doctor, one of the most sought-after bachelors in the city was a manipulative, sadistic bastard. She still couldn't believe she'd fallen for his solicitous support when he'd found out about Liana's condition a month after they'd broken up. During the two weeks doctors, including Brad, were working to give her sister every chance at recovery, he never brought up their relationship even though he'd sworn to get her back. He'd offered encouragement, a shoulder to lean on and a comforting embrace when the medical team announced there was nothing else they could do.

God, what a gullible fool she'd been. But never again. His threats could no longer force her to suffer a painful arm or wrist twist when she argued with him; she wouldn't have to try and dodge a fist to her abdomen or a kidney if she refused to sleep with him, and wouldn't have to suffer his touch or fake an orgasm under his thrusting body just to save herself a day or two of pain again.

Brad's morning surgery schedule gave her plenty of time to gather her belongings, but as Lillian entered the cold marble foyer, she wasted no time dashing upstairs to the master bedroom. In the walk-in closet, she grabbed the four-piece suitcase set she'd packed her clothes in a month ago and got to work without delay. Other than her wardrobe, toiletries and art supplies, she wanted nothing from this place.

Less than an hour later, she was brought to a sudden halt descending the stairs carrying the last of her paintings as Brad flung open the front door. The fury glittering in his cold brown eyes sent a frisson of alarm down her spine before she straightened and continued down the stairs. In the last month, she'd never cowered under that look and refused to start now.

With the sly calculation of a fox, Lillian watched his expression slide into one of feigned concern. "Baby, I'm so sorry about Liana. As soon as I got word, I cancelled the rest of my surgeries and rushed home to be here for you." He stepped forward as she reached the bottom of the stairs, not fooled in the least by his conciliatory tone or compassionate gaze. There was no way he'd come in through the front without noticing her packed car. "Taking those somewhere?" he asked, nodding toward the paintings tucked under her arms.

"Yes, out of here." She took a step sideways to go around him, but he followed, blocking her path. "Get out of my way, Brad. I'm leaving. Your threat to hurt Liana can no longer keep me here, as you damn well know."

In the blink of an eye, Brad reached for her upper arm, his demeanor changing back to frigidly furious. With her heart jumping into her throat, she leapt back, evaded his grip and sprinted toward the door only to have him halt her flight by grabbing a fistful of her hair. Painful pricks stabbed at her skull as several strands came ripping out as he flung her onto the floor, her hip exploding in agony when she landed on the unforgiving marble. Shock robbed her of breath as he lifted his foot and kicked her in the ribs, his assault coming so fast, and with first-time brutality, all she could do was lie there struggling to breathe through the waves of red-hot torment.

Squatting in front of her, it took every ounce of Lillian's battered control to keep from shrinking back as Brad brushed her hair aside with gentle fingers and said in a voice gone deceptively soft, "Baby, I thought we'd gotten past this penchant you have for thinking you can walk out on me. Don't you remember our first date, when I told you how much I was looking forward to a long relationship?"

Brad's eyes held the same cold, calculating gleam as when he'd whispered the numerous ways he could harm Liana while she lay helpless, ways no one would ever detect. He'd delivered that warning right in front of his medical colleagues in Liana's room, the look of caring concern reflected on his face never wavering. Only she had seen his eyes change and heard the menace in his voice.

But that was then, when Liana's fragile condition had left her no choice but to return to him, and stay in this house, under his thumb for the last four weeks. She had nothing left to lose by defying him except more pain, and she was in so much now, emotional and physical, Lillian was willing to risk more physical harm to get away from him once and for all.

"I remember," she whispered, allowing a small smile to curve her trembling lips as she lifted her face closer to his. "I also remember how your conceited, overbearing, possessive machinations drove me away." With a quick head butt, she sent him jerking backward enough for her to scramble to her feet. But it wasn't enough to get her to the door before he sent one picture flying out from under her arm with another grab.

How Lillian managed to retain her hold on the other when he backhanded her hard enough to slam her against the wall, splitting her lip and sending pain blossoming across the entire left side of her face, she didn't know. Gasping for breath, her head reeling as the jarring impact ricocheted in a burning agony across her ribcage, she let loose the building, consuming rage filling her.

"You bastard." Swinging the painting, one of her favorites, at his head with every ounce of strength she could muster, Lillian only had time for one deep, excruciating inhale as Brad stumbled against the entry table. Blood gushed from his temple where the corner of the frame had struck, his eyes widening in surprise as he crumpled to the floor.

With one arm cradling her ribs, she shuffled toward the door, the amount of blood pouring from his head adding nausea to her other afflictions. "Stay away from me, Doctor, or I'll file charges."

Brad greeted her threat with a pain-filled, scornful laugh. "You wouldn't dare. Who the fuck would believe you over me? In fact," he tried to get to his feet, failed and leaned against the wall, his face going from pale to chalk-white, "after I spin my side of this to Bryan, you'll be the one facing charges."

Even his over-protective cop brother wouldn't be able to deny the proof her pictures documented, so his threat didn't faze Lillian. She looked down at him with disdain, no longer fearing him as a strange calming numbness took over her body. "Did you honestly believe I would tolerate your abuse and threats without documenting every bruise? I took pictures of every mark you left on me and I won't hesitate to use them if you ever come near me again. Think your sterling reputation will hold up under such scrutiny? Goodbye, Brad."

Chalky with shock, dazed with grief and pain, Lillian couldn't think beyond the need to escape her anguish. She'd sublet her apartment when Brad had blackmailed her into moving in with him, putting everything she hadn't brought to his house and was now loaded in her car in storage. With no place to go, she ignored the warnings of her muddled reasoning that made the drastic decision to drive to the bank and clear out her checking and savings accounts ill-advised. With nothing left for her in the city she grew up in, she was determined to keep driving. Liana's body was already at the crematorium where her ashes would be stored in the mausoleum along with their parents, and she needed to find a way to come to peace with never getting the chance to tell her goodbye.

Tamping down on those crippling emotions, she refused to let them bubble to the surface as she veered onto the highway out of Salt Lake City with no destination in mind. Her whole body shook as the road stretched out before her. Wondering where she should go, she glanced at the bank bag bulging with cash. More tears cascaded down her face as she realized she would now inherit her sister's portion of their inheritance. Money wasn't a problem, but that offered no comfort for the heartache encompassing her.

At least Lillian was free of Brad, and this time for good. Not even his brother, whom she'd met once, could bail him out of this scrape if she chose to file charges. Ten years older than Brad, his brother bore part of the blame for Brad's behavior by always covering for him from as far back as when Brad had been a wild teenager. Between his colleagues and patients constant praise and admiration pumping up his God complex and Bryan still around to spoil him, she couldn't believe she'd ever fallen for his fake charm.

Nausea, blurred vision and excruciating discomfort forced

Lillian to stop as she crossed into Wyoming almost two hours later. She had no idea what town she was in when she pulled into a Walgreens and didn't care. After purchasing first aid supplies and dodging the solicitous inquiries from the salesclerk, she checked into the motel across the street for some much-needed rest.

Tossing her purchases onto a chair, she lay down on the bed intending to gather her thoughts before checking her injuries but couldn't stave off the stress induced exhaustion that pulled her under. She fell asleep with her sister's laughing face merging with Brad's furious image.

Lillian awoke to a pitch-black, strange room and a myriad of aches and pains. Rolling over, she winced, the pain radiating around her ribcage bringing clarification to her groggy, jumbled senses. *Liana.* A sob caught in her throat as she sat up and flicked on the bedside light. Blinking, she realized one eye wouldn't open fully. *Brad.* A surge of anger tightened her muscles as she stood on wobbly legs. Vacillating between gut-clenching grief and a slow-burning fury, she padded into the miniscule bathroom, turned on the light and groaned out loud at her image in the mirror. Her topsy-turvy emotional imbalance took second place to the distress of seeing just how hard Brad had struck her.

Turning away from the view of her swollen black eye, cut puffy lip and bruised cheek, she retrieved the first aid supplies and did her best to doctor her injuries. It was too late for an icepack on her face to do much good, but the medicated salve eased the sting in her lip and from the small nick near her eye. Lifting her sweatshirt, she winced at the purple splotches forming under her breasts. The smart thing would be to find an emergency room and get x-rays, but her breathing wasn't compromised, indicating no punctured lung, and she figured she could wrap her ribs as well as a professional.

The urge to get going, to put as much distance between her and the place she could never call home again, pounded at her temples. Lillian wrapped bandages around her ribcage and used medical tape to hold them snug, surprised by the relief the slight pressure gave her. It wasn't much, but along with downing three extra-strength aspirin, the pain was now manageable. She ran a brush through her tangled, auburn hair and brushed her teeth before stepping out into the frigid early morning air. After checking out of the motel carrying a to-go cup of steaming coffee offered by the worried looking receptionist, she got on the road again, figuring she would stop when her body insisted, or she needed gas.

The desolate winter prairieland matched her bleak mood as she traveled north through Wyoming while replaying happy memories of her and Liana's childhood; their first day of school when Lillian had shoved the boy who'd pulled Liana's braid and made her cry; the time they'd gone bike riding and ventured too far from home, getting themselves lost until well after dark and the police found them; their double date to their Junior prom where they'd indulged in alcohol for the first time and ended up grounded for a month; the fun they'd had on their college spring break trip to Padre Island.

Heavy, grief-laden despair pressed down on her chest as she passed a herd of snow-encrusted, slow-lumbering bison traversing across a snow packed plateau. She shivered and nudged the heat up a notch as the thick gray clouds spit small flakes on her windshield. Liana used to love snow and catching Lillian unaware with a snowball to the back of the head. God, she would get pissed whenever her sister's aim was spot on. As she reached the Montana border, her low gas gauge pinged, forcing her to find a gas station and take a break.

Despite her aches and pains making themselves known with throbbing intensity and the dark clouds swirling ahead, threatening more snow, Lillian got back in her car after filling up and drove on. *Not yet*, she thought, *the memories are still too close.* Her trek made no sense, but neither did her sister's death at the age of thirty-four. Weren't they just laughing about growing old together as two, eccentric spinsters a few weeks ago? With Liana's nose always buried in a book she was editing and Lillian's focus glued to her current painting, it was a wonder either of them had ever set aside their absorption with their work long enough to accept a date.

Lillian's mouth curled in a derisive sneer as she recalled what the last date she'd accepted had led to. No fancy dinner or the mediocre pleasure of an orgasm was worth wasting her time. Give her a glass of wine and her pretty pink vibrator and she was content. There was no way she would relinquish control over her life again, especially not now, when there was no one left she cared enough about to sacrifice for. A pang gripped her abdomen at the reminder of how alone she was now, her gaze turning watery again.

Eight hours, two pit stops, three cups of coffee, one candy bar and a steady amount of snowfall later, Lillian passed a sign showing ten miles to the Billings, Montana exit. Figuring that was as good a place as any to spend the night, she slowed to a crawl, the winter storm that was closer than she'd guessed turning into a white sheet of windblown swirls. She was no novice to traveling alone having flown around the country and elsewhere for art shows by herself for the last eight years, nor was this the first time she'd driven with snow falling hard enough to warrant caution.

But it didn't take long for Lillian's first experience in leaving behind everything that was familiar to her, along with driving through a slow-building snowstorm sweeping across a wide-open, barren expanse of nothingness to turn treacherous. Controlling the car against the buffeting wind and slick roads zapped what little strength she had left after traveling all day and shunning food due to lingering nausea. The ten miles to the turnoff she kept an eye out for seemed to go on forever, the traffic on the now snow-hidden highway dwindling from sparse to almost nonexistent over the next thirty minutes. With no sign of another advertised turnoff, she took a wild guess born of worry and fatigue and opted for the next exit.

Gripping the wheel with sweaty palms, Lillian turned onto a much narrower road, hoping it would take her into Billings, figuring it couldn't be that far. Right now, she would welcome the sight of any building, or heck, even another vehicle. At least her snow tires were holding out, helping her through the slow build-up. Her heater worked well and she was sure the spare blanket was still stowed in the trunk, if she needed it. That didn't keep the tremors of unease from invading her sore, depleted body as her head grew fuzzy with disorientation from the blinding white terrain filling her vision no matter which direction she looked.

Staying along the wooded tree line helped guide her, but with darkness fast approaching and the constant struggle to stay focused, Lillian had just decided to stop and hope for a signal on her phone when a large, leggy elk darted out from the trees. *Talk about startled like a deer caught in the headlights.* She didn't have time to giggle about that thought as her attempted swerve to miss the animal sent the car into a spin as slow and sluggish as her brain, the uncontrollable, rotating glide ending with the front end buried up to the windshield in a ten-foot snow bank.

With a frustrated swing and exasperated huff, Mitchell buried his ax in the wood stump and shook his head in disbelief. What the hell was someone doing driving a sporty Mazda Miata on a Montana back road during a raging snowstorm? They were lucky their inevitable stranded predicament occurred near his cabin, that he happened to be here and outside getting wood to witness their loss of control through the trees separating his place from the road. Yanking his sheepskin lined coat closed and his Stetson down to shield his eyes from the blowing snow, it was too bad he didn't get to share in the occupant's luck.

Mitchell trudged through the piling snow, bemoaning the loss of his solitude for the next few days. Given the weather and the distance between his cabin and the nearest towns of Billings and

Willow Springs, it looked like he would have a guest for the next few days. He wasn't happy about that; the month of February was still difficult for him two years following his wife, Abbie's lost battle with cancer. This was his first winter in Montana, and he'd been looking forward to these few days away from his new practice as the encroaching memories pushed the heartache he kept tucked away to the surface.

Tabling his irritation, he breathed a sigh of relief for the break in heavy snowfall as he emerged from the woods and sloughed through the already several feet of cold accumulation toward the stranded car still puffing out exhaust from the running engine. The lull wouldn't last, so it was imperative he get the occupants back to his place as quickly as possible.

The driver's side door creaked open as he reached the back end, his annoyance with the woman struggling to release her seatbelt dropping away when he eyed her pale, bruised face. The car hadn't landed buried in the snow wall with enough impact to open the airbag, and the snug fit of the seatbelt would have prevented those injuries from happening just now.

Mitchell got to the open door as she emerged, her gasp of pain as she bent over with an arm wrapped around her upper waist prompting him to reach for her sweater-covered arm. "Sit down. You are not going to get sick or pass out." He pressed on her shoulder until her butt returned to the seat, her booted feet buried up to her calves in the snow. She was alone in the car, which made it easier on him to have to deal with only one unwelcome guest.

To his surprise, she glared up at him out of dark purple eyes, shaking her cloud of deep auburn hair out of her face as she snapped, "Says who?"

I'm not only stuck with a houseguest, but one with attitude, yet another pesky irritation. "Me." Squatting in front of her to block the wind, he cupped her chin with a gloved hand and held her still as he examined her black eye, swollen face and cut mouth, his hand tightening at the obvious signs of abuse. "Let me guess. You walked into a door," he drawled, figuring she would skirt the truth like most abused women.

She jerked her head and he released her to keep from causing her more stress. Her lips curled in derision as she replied, "Yeah, a door with fists."

Her honesty surprised Mitchell and earned her brownie points despite the sarcasm. He nodded, the hot ball of anger coiling in his gut the same response he'd experienced with every case of abuse admitted into the trauma center in Denver he had headed for five years. Pushing to his feet, he curtailed the desire to question her and searched for a coat among the belongings piled on the back seat. "I can check you over at my cabin, just through the woods. Can you make it that far?"

She frowned, her eyes turning wary as she cast a look around at their desolate surroundings. "I can if I have to, but it would be foolish to follow a stranger to a secluded cabin in the woods."

"And it wasn't foolish to drive in this weather in a vehicle ill-equipped to handle it without ending up like this?" he returned dryly. "I'm cold and the heavy shit will start up again any moment. I'll give you two minutes to talk to the sheriff in Willow Springs and then I'm hauling ass back to my place, with or without you." Digging his satellite phone out of the heavy coat pocket, he punched in Grayson Monroe's direct number, praying he caught him in. When he answered, he gave his friend a quick rundown and then thrust the phone toward her, swearing as he noticed the blue tinge to her lips despite the heat blowing inside the still idling car and his position blocking the wind. "Make it fast."

Chapter 2

Lillian worked at concentrating on the deep voice resonating through the satellite phone her reluctant rescuer handed her, but it continued to be *his* gruff but concerned tone bouncing around in her head. His stern, quiet insistence she would not get sick had irritated her since he couldn't possibly expect the nauseous bile in her throat to subside simply because he insisted. Only it had, and that was just as annoying.

"You'll be fine with Dr. Hoffstetter, a lot better off than where you're at now. Go with him and I'll get a tow truck out there as soon as possible."

Great, I have no choice but to trust a cop and doctor. What were the freaking odds of that irony? Closing her eyes, Lillian fought to get herself under control. The sheriff clicked off, leaving her no doubt he expected her to believe him and that he was about as happy with her circumstances as the tall, rugged cowboy doctor staring down at her with impatience stamped on his face. She couldn't see his eyes shielded by the lowered brim of his hat, but there was no mistaking his taut jaw. The salt and pepper goatee framing his mouth drew her eyes to the tight press of his lips.

Left with no choice, she handed him the phone and nodded. "I can make it to your cabin. Thank you."

"I'll grab your coat," he replied, working the back door open. "Anything else will have to wait a few hours, or maybe until morning."

Lillian picked up the bank bag, sucked in a deep breath and pushed to her feet, the throbbing tenderness of her ribs making itself known again. Holding out her hip-length, all-weather coat, the astute doctor asked, "He got you in the ribs also, didn't he?"

"Yes, but I'm okay." Shrugging on the coat, she zipped it up, feeling warmer already.

"Let's hope so." Closing the car door, he took her arm and steered her toward the trees. "Walk in my path. It'll be easier for you."

She did, keeping her eyes down and placing her feet in the deep prints left from his trek to the car. The woods offered a small break from the cold wind and they emerged a few minutes later into a clearing. She was so cold and miserable, not to mention aching from head to toe that not even a five-star hotel could look as inviting as the rustic cabin with smoke billowing from the chimney. The doctor's calm silence, towering height and large frame offered a comfort she didn't think she'd needed.

Ushering her inside, he shut the door just as the heavy snowfall returned with near whiteout intensity. "Sit down and let me look at your ribs."

So much for the comfort she'd been experiencing. His brusque, no-nonsense manner rubbed her wrong – she'd had enough of bossy men in the past month to last her a lifetime. "I appreciate your rescue," she forced herself to say in a neutral tone, "but as I've said, I'm fine."

Turning from her, he hung his coat and hat on hooks by the door, peeled off his gloves and tossed them on the table and then faced her again with his fists going to his lean hips. At five-eight, Lillian had never considered herself short, but she'd never had to crane her head back to look so far up at someone before. His thick hair matched his goatee in color, mostly silver with hints of black interspersed, and was worn long enough to curl around the collar of his dark green flannel shirt. She'd assumed his bulky coat accounted for the breadth of his shoulders, but she was wrong. His height made him appear on the lean side, but there was no mistaking the ripped, bulging muscles in his thighs as he stepped in front of her or along his hair-sprinkled forearms as he shoved up his sleeves to just below his elbows.

Cupping her chin in his warm palm, she wasn't prepared for the jolt his tightened hold gave her. "Have you been checked out by a medical professional?"

No, I just ran from the painful heartbreak. Lillian realized the physical distance she had put between her and Salt Lake City did nothing to help her escape from the agonizing sorrow of Liana's passing followed by the harrowing distress of Brad's possessive temper. His point-blank question left her no room for evasion, and she wouldn't lie. All she wanted from him right now was a few moments to lie down and gather her thoughts.

"No, I haven't had time, but…"

"Then sit down and lift your sweater so I can check you over. Sheriff Monroe told you I'm a doctor." Before she could blink, he divested her of her coat and pressed her shoulders until she landed on the edge of the double bed, the only piece of furniture in the miniscule cabin other than the small table, two chairs and a recliner facing the fireplace. "I'm Mitchell Hoffstetter. What's your name?"

"Lillian, and this isn't necessary. I'm breathing fine." *Maybe a little heavier than usual*, she puzzled over as he reached for the hem of her sweater and her breathing sped up. She must be more tired than she thought if she could get flustered by this polite, but not so welcoming stranger.

Ignoring her, he remained every inch the professional as he pushed her sweater above her chest and picked up her right hand to place on the bunched-up top. "Hold it up while I unwrap you. Did you do this, or did someone help you?"

I don't have anyone anymore. She bit her lip to stop tears from forming in her eyes and gave up the ridiculous battle of trying to keep his hands off her that was costing her too much energy. "I did, yesterday."

Mitchell tossed aside the tape and swore as he saw the purple bruising that hurt her so much. His touch was gentle as he palpated her ribs but the discomfort was enough to elicit a gasp of pain. "Sorry, pet," he murmured, the low-voiced, distracted comment grating on her nerves.

"I'm not a damn dog," Lillian returned, shifting away from his probing fingers.

Looking down at her, he cocked his head and stepped back, his intent gaze drawing a shiver that had nothing to do with being chilled. "Do you have a dislike of nicknames?"

"No, just of the men who use them," she retorted.

"So you prefer women, but it wasn't a woman who knocked you around."

Exasperated, she blew out a breath and yanked her sweater down. "I didn't before, but I just might learn to swing that way. Are you done poking at me?"

Mitchell's amused grin reached his eyes. "Yes, and I didn't feel a fracture. You'll heal better without wrapping but you can ice them while I heat up something for dinner. When was the last time you ate?"

"Earlier today." Lillian didn't mention she'd only eaten a candy bar.

He turned to rummage through a cupboard above the sink. The apartment sized refrigerator with an upper freezer and stove along the wall was the extent of the kitchen. "I see I'm going to have to make sure my questions are specific. What have you eaten since this incident occurred?" He extracted a tube of antibiotic ointment and padded back over to the bed, his probing gaze once again on her face.

"Are you this bossy with all your patients? If so, I can't imagine too many of them come back for a second appointment." His interrogation might stem from professional concern but coming on the heels of getting free of Brad's abusive hold on her, the constant questions grated on her already strung tight nerves.

"I don't care about signing you on as a new patient, only about not being forced to get an air ambulance out here in the next twenty-four hours. Hold still while I apply this ointment to your cuts."

Well, that certainly put me in my place. Guilt slid through her; she'd never thought of that. She held her breath as he rubbed the medicine onto the cut by her eye and then on her lip, his touch light but enough to warm her, or maybe she was just feverish from her injuries and exhaustion. Yes, that must be it because there was no way she was attracted to him, despite his rugged good looks and a body any red-blooded woman would drool over.

He stepped back and she stood, a sudden, room-spinning swirl of dizziness assailing her, forcing her to grab Mitchell's shoulders. She closed her eyes against the sharp concern in his gaze as he gripped her hips and eased her back down onto the bed.

"Again, what have you eaten today?" he demanded. "Or, do you have other injuries I can't see?"

Sighing, she opened her eyes to his face hovering right above hers, his warm breath wafting across her lips. She wondered if he included some of that bossiness in his kisses and then questioned what the heck was wrong with her to have such a thought pop into her fuzzy head. "A candy bar," she admitted, leaving out her bruised hip and leaning back to restore her bearings.

"Figures. Stay still while I heat something up."

Mitchell kept his annoyance under wraps as he turned on the propane fired stove and retrieved the packaged chicken breasts from the refrigerator. So much for enjoying a peaceful few days in front of the fire, away from the demands of his job and the well-meaning but nosy friends he'd made since answering the ad for a family doctor in the small town of Willow Springs. At the time, he'd thought the much slower pace would suit him, that trading the big, noisy city for a quiet, rural environment would soothe his heartbreak faster. He didn't have the day to day memories haunting him here like in Denver where he saw Abbie's face in every room of their home, heard her engaging laugh every time he ate at a restaurant they had frequented and pictured her writhing, glistening bare body at the BDSM club where they'd met.

But it hadn't taken him long to discover he couldn't flee the pain of losing her. Abbie's sweet, biddable nature had drawn on his dominant urges and when she had submitted to him the first night they'd met, there'd been no looking back, or elsewhere for either of them. Eight years hadn't been enough time with her, and too often he found himself resenting her for leaving him, followed by a stab of guilt from that emotional buffer.

Was it too much to ask for these few days alone so he could wallow in self-pity and rage at fate for the last two years of loneliness and sorrow?

The single overhead bulb flickered and then went out, plunging the cabin into semi-darkness, the gray cast from the one window and amber/yellow glow of burning embers in the fireplace the only sources shedding any light. Lillian didn't say anything, which prompted him to look around and check on her. Slumped over on the bed, she lay sound asleep, her slim legs still dangling over the side, her upper body twisted at an uncomfortable angle. Grateful for the few minutes reprieve, he slid the pan off the burner, the generator kicking in as he shrugged his coat and gloves back on. At least he had stacked enough wood by the door to last a while before her presence had interrupted him.

Thirty minutes later, wood sat piled next to the fireplace and Mitchell was setting the fried chicken and a bowl of corn on the table when his guest roused. He watched her stretch and then wince as she arched back too far. Her grimace was enough to set aside the fleeting appreciation of eyeing her movements that pushed her breasts upward and shifted those long, slender legs apart. The woman looked good in snug denim.

Mitchell shoved that observance to the back of his mind in favor of getting a hot meal down her. "I would ask how long you've gone without sleep, but I won't bother. Come eat something."

Lillian sat up and scrubbed her hands over her face, mumbling, "I'm not hungry."

"You're irritating me, pet." She glared at him, her eyes flashing. Why he enjoyed riling her with the nickname, he didn't know, and he didn't care for the way her censuring look stirred his cock.

"And you're irritating me with your nagging, but we're stuck with each other for now, aren't we?" Lifting her hands, she tunneled long fingers through her hair, pushing the thick, dark red tangled mass back, offering him an unobstructed view of her pale face.

"We are." He pointed to a chair. "Come on. You need protein, and then I'll put an ice pack on your ribs."

She shuddered, standing up. Plopping into the chair, she cast him a derisive look. "I have enough reminders of why I have sworn off men. You don't need to add to them."

Mitchell took the vacant seat across the small table from her, stabbed a plump chicken breast and reached over to dump it on her plate. "Not all men are like the one who gave you those bruises, but I'm fine with you including me in the group you've sworn off of."

Frowning, Lillian picked up the fork and knife and cut into the chicken, ignoring him as he scooped corn onto her plate before seeing to his own servings. The fire crackled as the wind rattled the window and door, picking up speed while they ate in silence. Mitchell liked she didn't feel the need to chit chat, but the longer he surveyed her black eye, bruised cheek and cut lip, the more his curiosity and ire increased until he couldn't hold back from getting answers.

"Tell me why you didn't seek medical attention instead of driving into a forecasted snowstorm."

Lillian swallowed, looking up at him with a smooth expression. "Because I'm an idiot?"

He shrugged. The girl had grit, he'd give her that. "I don't know enough to answer that. Enlighten me." Instead, she shoveled in a forkful of corn, her slim brows dipping in a frown he found as cute as the freckles sprinkled across her slim, straight nose.

"Why are you staring at me like that?" she asked, tilting her head so her hair swept over her shoulder and upper arm.

"I find you attractive even if your intrusion on my privacy doesn't sit well with me. The least you can do for your imposition is tell me why you ended up stranded in the middle of the state." He could tell she didn't know how to take his blunt honesty.

Her gaze flickered out the window as the wind howled and the snow changed to ice pellets pinging against the glass. "Aren't you worried about the weather?" Lillian swung her eyes back to him. "For that matter, why are you out in the middle of nowhere in this kind of weather?"

"No, to your first question. The cabin may look rustic, but it's sound, the generator will hold up, I have enough firewood and food to last a week and friends who know where I am and a way to contact them if I need help. I grew up in Denver and spent a lot of time at my cabin in the mountains, so I'm used to making do during rougher weather. Why do you keep answering my questions with a question?" Mitchell grabbed another piece of chicken and held it up, offering it to her first. She shook her head and he didn't push it since she'd polished off a whole breast and was finishing the corn.

Reaching for the glass of water he'd poured for her, she took a long drink before saying, "I just spent a month unable to go anywhere, answer a call or get on the computer without a guy interrogating me. Excuse me if I'm not inclined to go down that path again."

Mitchell drilled her with a pointed look. "The same guy who took his fist to you?"

A rueful grin lifted her mouth. "Try a hefty, backhanded swing, and yes, same asshole."

He already knew the answer but asked anyway. "It wasn't the first time, was it?"

Lillian blew out a breath, her hand tightening on her napkin as she picked it up. "No, but it's not what you're thinking. I didn't stay out of some misplaced denial or because I believed he didn't mean to hurt me. And it's none of your business so that's all I'm saying about it."

There was more, the reason she put up with the man until recently was portrayed in her bleak expression and sorrow-filled eyes. But she was right, he didn't need to know the specifics to offer her a safe place to stay until the weather let up. He didn't have to like it, but there was no sense in bemoaning what couldn't be changed.

Noticing her long blinks, he stood and picked up their empty plates. "Good enough. If you're done, I'll give you a shirt to sleep in and an ice pack for your ribs." When she didn't argue he realized her fatigue went bone-deep. More answers would have to wait until morning.

"How can I sleep with a cold icepack? I'm already chilled." Lillian pushed back from the table and rose, reaching for the shirt Mitchell handed her.

"I'll time it for ten minutes. That will have to do until morning. The cold would have been more effective within hours of your injury, so you'll only get minimal relief using it now." He nodded toward the only other room in the cabin. "The bathroom is over there but there's not a lot of hot water stored, so go easy please. And don't linger while I get the icepack wrapped in a towel or it will melt and won't be any good to you."

"I'm too tired to do anything except wash my face and change. If we're sharing the bed, fair warning – I'm used to sleeping alone and having the covers to myself."

Mitchell watched her flounce into the bathroom and shut the door, admiring her gumption and easy acceptance of the limited sleeping space. When confronted with sharing a bed with a stranger, most women would balk and at least try to argue for an alternative. He might find her physically attractive and her tart personality cute for now, but he had the control both age and being an experienced Dom afforded him. That control, along with his morose mood meant she was perfectly safe from fending off any sexual passes. In another time, maybe another place, he might not be averse to stripping her out of those jeans and demonstrating where her attitude could land her or the difference between harmful abusive pain and erotic torment.

Lillian wouldn't admit it to Doctor Mitchell Hoffstetter, but she felt better after eating. Staring at her pathetic reflection in the bathroom mirror, she could tolerate how awful she looked now the dizziness had cleared. If she weren't still so tired, she might give in to the temptation to continue sparring with her host. There was something about his deep, commanding voice that helped keep her mind off the worrisome building snowstorm and her sorrow over Liana's passing. For the first time in her life, she was truly alone and that both scared her and made her sad. As annoying as she found him, Mitchell's bossiness was still preferable to silence and her depressing thoughts.

But even after that quick nap, fatigue weighed her down and she longed to escape her sorrow and aches through sleep. After stripping off her jeans and sweater, she pulled on the blue flannel shirt he loaned her, the hem falling to mid-thigh, the sleeves needing rolled up several times. It was wide enough to wrap around her twice, but warm and comfortable, and that's all she cared about. The slight woodsy odor reminded her of him as she left the bathroom, his direct, observant gaze as she padded over to the bed warming her insides. Yes, she mused, slipping under the turned down covers, she was definitely exhausted if a stranger she didn't particularly care for could stir her up with a look.

"Are you sure I need that?" She eyed the wrapped ice with a shiver as he approached the bed.

"Yes." Instead of giving it to her, Mitchell delved under the blanket, and the shirt and placed the cold compress against her ribcage where she was the sorest. "How's that?" he asked, stepping back and flipping the covers back up.

"Freakin' cold, how do you think it is?" She sounded bitchy but damn, it was cold.

"Be careful, pet, or you won't like the way I warm you up."

She gritted her teeth at the nickname. "Is that a threat? I thought I could trust you?"

"I don't threaten, just warn. Remember that and we'll get along fine. I also don't hit, but I do have ways to punish a woman you wouldn't care for."

He turned from her but she wasn't about to let that go. Burying deeper into the comfortable bed, she whispered on a tired sigh, "What do you mean, women like me?"

Mitchell settled in the recliner and pulled a book out of the side pocket, flicking her a look of exasperation. "Never mind. Go to sleep, Lillian."

Her eyes drifted closed of their own accord, rousing sometime later from the loud crackle of logs added to the fire. The ice pack was no longer nestled under the shirt, its removal without her waking proving how deeply she'd slept but not for how long. The room was dark except for the glow from the fire where her eyes focused as soon as she lifted her lids. In appreciative silence, she gazed upon Mitchell's bare back as he bent to remove his jeans. It didn't surprise her to see he went commando, or to note his lean muscled body was as pleasurable to look at as she'd imagined. Those broad shoulders tapered to a narrow waist and taut buttocks topped his long, muscled legs.

He turned, lifting an inquisitive brow at catching her staring. "You must not be as out of it as I'd thought."

"I've sworn off men but I'm not dead, at least I don't think so." If he wasn't going to act prudish then neither would she, but *holy moly*, the man had an impressive package and build.

"No, you're not," he replied, strolling around to the other side with complete disregard for his nudity. "Go back to sleep. I won't bother you."

Bummer. Lillian drifted back to sleep as the bed dipped with his weight, a giggle lodged in her throat from that one-word, wayward thought.

She slept through the snowstorm as it raged into a full-blown blizzard, the snow piling up past the one window over the next few hours. She didn't wake up when Mitchell did, or when he dressed and started bacon sizzling on the stove. His conversation with the sheriff via his satellite phone went unheard, the coffee aroma didn't tickle her sense of smell. It wasn't until mid-morning when her body's demand for the restroom won out over some explicit dreams that she rolled out from her warm cocoon, shivering from head to toe as her bare feet hit the wood floor.

Blinking to clear her sleepy vision, the first thing to come into focus was Mitchell sitting at the table appearing content and well-rested as he finished off the last bite of scrambled eggs. With the images of her writhing under the forceful plunges of his thrusting body still playing through her head, Lillian found herself resenting his probing once-over out of eyes mostly green this morning with the yellow glow of the fire haloing his head. She had zip-zero interest in men before Liana collapsed in a coma six weeks ago, and even less than that, if possible, by the time she left Brad's house without looking back. Her appreciation of the doctor's rescue, hospitality and physical attributes she understood, but not her mind and body betraying her with those dreams that stirred up her libido.

"Good morning. You slept well, so why the scowl?" Mitchell stood and picked up his plate, carrying it over to the sink.

"Maybe I'm not a morning person. Excuse me." She walked into the bathroom where she washed up and dressed. A shower could wait until later. Right now it was more important to shield her body from the appreciative glance he'd given her bare legs and to get herself under control. *It's the circumstances that have thrown us together in close proximity and my stress, that's all this is*, she insisted before opening the door to see him setting a plate piled with eggs and bacon on the table. Feeling irritable, she grumbled, "I'm not hungry. You eat it."

With a sigh, he stalked around the table and peered down at her with a frown. "You need fuel to heal. Quit being so stubborn." Of course her stomach took that moment to rumble in hunger. A taunting smile appeared as he cocked his head. "It seems I know your body's needs better than you, baby."

Lillian reacted without thinking, hearing him call her baby igniting her temper with the flashback of Brad's sneering voice. Lifting her arm, she swung only to have him halt her slap before her palm connected with his face. He gripped her wrist, his hold loose but unbreakable. his eyes going to narrowed slits and boring into hers. She sucked in a trembling breath, shaken by the force of her anger.

"You really do have a deep-rooted aversion to affectionate nicknames, don't you?" he murmured.

"Especially that one," she returned without thinking, the information revealing in its simplicity.

He held her in his penetrating perusal and light grip for several seconds before releasing her from both with a short nod. "Understood. Sit down and eat before it gets cold."

Mitchell waited until Lillian complied, sat down and picked up her fork before turning his back on her. He had seen the second the word 'baby' triggered something inside her, her reaction as volatile as his thoughts. The urge to poke at her for more information about this guy and the circumstances responsible for her landing here was as strong as the desire to hunt him down and exact retribution for her. The intensity of his need to do those two things bothered him. Not since his wife, Abbie had been diagnosed with stage four cancer had he experienced such a profound desire to right the wrong done to a woman. He didn't even know Lillian, not like he had Abbie, or the submissive members of The Barn, the private BDSM club he'd joined eight months ago, shortly after arriving in Willow Springs. With any of them, he could indulge in a long spank-session over his knees to get the answers he wanted and then reward them with a climax when they quit holding back.

Stoking the fire, a warm curl of remembered fondness spread around his chest as the memory of Abbie coming to stand before him with a shy smile popped up. Spanking for discipline or to get answers was sometimes necessary, but nothing beat the pleasure of watching your sub approach you with need of your hard hand connecting with their bare flesh reflected on their face. It hadn't taken long to convince Abbie not to wait for his order if she yearned for the release his butt-reddening smacks could give her and he had loved watching as she would pull down her pants and drape herself over his lap without words.

Swiveling his head, he watched Lillian eat with her brows dipped in a frown. This woman didn't possess a submissive bone in her slender body, that he could detect anyway. It wouldn't do to fantasize about pulling answers from her the old-fashioned way. The storm had abated early this morning and street crews would head out later today and into tomorrow. After assuring Grayson they were both fine, the sheriff put digging out her car as low priority and would let him know when they could get to it in a day or two. After that, he and his attractive but annoying houseguest would go their separate ways and the concerns he harbored for her would go away as fast as she'd interrupted his solitude.

Until then, all Mitchell had to do was ignore the odd itch to erase the sadness lurking in her extraordinary eyes that mimicked his sorrow when he thought of Abbie. As much as he disliked seeing those bruises marring her face, the fleeting idea of replacing her bad memories with one fucking good one before they parted company wouldn't come to pass. Since losing his wife, he only indulged his dominant sexual preferences with submissive women at the club, ones who didn't expect anything other than his undivided attention for a scene or two.

It was best not to involve himself with Lillian's troubles other than to get her well enough to send her on her way to wherever she was headed in a few days.

Chapter 3

"The storm has passed, but I told Sheriff Monroe to put digging your car out as low priority." Lillian picked up her plate and stood, her mouth tightening with pique as she flicked Mitchell an irritated look. He held up a hand to ward off her complaint. "We're both fine here for another twenty-four hours, and even longer if necessary. There are others in worse straits, including livestock that local ranchers could use a helping hand in getting to."

Her shoulders slumped as she carried her empty dish to the sink. He liked she didn't expect him to clean up after her.

"You're right. Even though this is my first winter storm outside of the city, I should have realized the efforts it takes to get to people who are so spread out." She rinsed her plate and turned to lean against the counter. "I missed the turnoff to Billings, where I planned to stop. Where is this Willow Springs you mentioned?"

"Not far, closer than Billings from here. Hailing from Denver, it took me some time to get used to the small-town vibes, but now I like it. If you're in no hurry, you should stay a few days to rest up and let yourself heal."

A sorrowful spasm crossed her face before she averted her head toward the snow-covered window. "I might, seeing as I'm not headed anywhere in particular. I wish I had my paints," she murmured with a soft sigh.

"You're an artist? I wondered when I saw the canvases in the back of your car." Mitchell walked over to a cupboard to her left and retrieved a notebook of unlined, blank sheets. His arm brushed hers as he lowered it and handed her the tablet. "You can have this to sketch in, if you want. It'll give you something to do while I go out and clear the window and get more wood. There should be some pencils or pens in that drawer." He nodded to the end drawer along the counter.

For the first time, her eyes shone with gratitude and pleasure as she took the simple offering, careful not to let their hands touch. "Thank you."

"You're welcome. I want to check your ribs before I go out." Michell wiggled his fingers in an upward motion, signaling for her to lift her sweater. This time, her deep purple gaze lit with amusement.

"Men usually don't insist on me making it easy for them to get under my clothes."

His mouth twitched, enjoying her humor. It was so much better than her sniping or sadness. "I'm not most men and I'm checking you out as a doctor, not a lover."

She set the tablet on the counter and lifted her sweater, her eyes on his face as she smirked, "So you're not imagining what I look like without my bra right now?"

Sliding his eyes down, he visually caressed her white satin-covered breasts long enough to watch her nipples pucker in response. "About as much as you're not imagining me touching you." Her eyes flashed and she started to lower her top. Apparently she could dish it out but had trouble taking it. Or maybe she was fighting her response as hard as he was struggling to suppress the growing need to ease the pain reflected on her face with something pleasurable. He stopped her by reaching out and running his fingers over her bruised ribs. "Relax. It's just a little harmless banter to break up the tedium."

Lillian sucked in a deep breath as he lightly probed her black and blue ribcage. "Do you always blow so hot and cold? One minute you're the nice, concerned doctor, the next a put-upon host and now the congenial acquaintance."

"I could say the same about you, pet," he answered absently as he tried to palpate her ribs without causing her too much discomfort. When he realized he let slip with another nickname, he glanced at her face, lifting one brow at her silence.

After a moment, she shrugged, saying, "Just don't call me baby."

"Deal. One to ten, how sore are you?"

"Maybe a four or five. I'm fine."

He lowered his hand, replying, "You will be in a few weeks. Until then, no lifting or straining. I have aspirin, if you need it." He plucked it out of an upper cabinet and set the bottle on the counter and then strode toward the door to shrug into his coat. "This will take a while, so rest and amuse yourself until I come back in." Snatching up his gloves, he stepped out into bright sunshine but frigid cold air, wondering at the urge to put space between them.

Lillian scowled at the closed door. Mitchell's parting comment had sounded more like an order than a suggestion, his clipped tone stirring up her resentment of this whole situation. When she'd teased him about getting under her clothes, she'd done so to throw him off guard, the same as her lightning quick, warm responses to his innocent touches had flustered her. The same desperate impulse to drive away and keep on going that had gripped her when she'd stumbled out of Brad's house returned to plague her. Only she was as stuck here, with no way out as much as she had been trapped for the previous month into staying with Brad.

Liana's smiling face popped up into Lillian's head as she remembered their laughter as they'd tossed tinsel they'd plucked off their Christmas tree onto each other. That was the last time she'd heard Liana's voice. A week later, Lillian had gotten the phone call from her sister's boss telling her she'd collapsed at work and was en route to the hospital.

Blinking back tears, Lillian sat at the table and started sketching the scene in her head. During her two-week vigilance at the hospital, she'd passed the time by drawing childhood memories of the two of them, thinking they might help Liana heal when she awoke. After her twin had been moved to the care home and Brad blackmailed Lillian with threats to her beloved sister, she'd been too distraught and then too angry with him and fate to sketch any more memories.

It had been a grave mistake to let herself lean on Brad right after Liana had collapsed. She'd broken up with him because of his high-handed, possessive manner and attempts to control her, but the shock and despair of her sister's condition had rendered her helpless to cope alone. With no other family, Brad had taken advantage of her grief and uncertainty and then revealed the true depth of his obsession with her when she'd backed away. But every snide, cutting remark, every punch, arm twist, kick and unwanted fuck had been worth it to ensure Liana didn't suffer at his hands. Lillian still shuddered when she recalled the things he'd said he could do to her, things sure to cause tremendous pain without anyone being the wiser.

A scraping sound drew her eyes to the window as she finished a sketch of Liana reaching to place the star on a Christmas tree. She watched the snow fall away from the window, one scrape from top to bottom at a time, until enough cleared she could see Mitchell. A black Stetson covered his head and a scarf tucked around his neck was stretched over his mouth and nose, but there was no mistaking that unnerving, penetrating gaze zeroing in on her through the cleared glass. She wanted to look away, to hide from whatever he was trying to calculate from her expression but refused to back down.

And then his head moved in an almost imperceptible nod, as if he'd been checking up on her and affirmed she was doing his bidding by resting and drawing. She slid her eyes away from the window, a curl of resentment forming a knot in her stomach. *He's a doctor, I should cut him some slack.* Maybe she would if she hadn't been forced to endure another doctor's insufferable dictates for weeks. Mitchell's tendency to order instead of ask might stem from medical concern, but she didn't care. The part of her that still trembled whenever she thought of Brad's retribution when she didn't meet his demands insisted she retaliate.

With no thought in mind except to venture outside in a small show of rebellion, Lillian tried not to think about her aching face and ribs as she tugged on her boots after Mitchell moved away from the window. Snatching her coat off the rack, she buttoned up and pulled on her gloves, figuring she wouldn't mind if the cold air numbed her face. Opening the door, she shielded her eyes against the glare of bright sunshine bouncing off a field of winter white.

The sound of an ax cutting through wood resonated from around the side and Lillian trudged through several feet of snow to spy on her host, admiring the glistening icicles dangling from frozen tree limbs. Peeking around the corner, she spotted Mitchell, now coatless, lifting an ax above his head and bringing it down in the center of a propped-up log, his strong swing splitting the wood in two. *Okay, he is worth staring at*, she admitted as his shoulder and back muscles bunched under the brown flannel shirt. Snug jeans emphasized the clench of taut buttocks as he replaced the split pieces with another hefty log. He was just as eye-catching now as last night when she'd seen his naked body silhouetted by the glowing fire. She might have been groggy with lingering exhaustion, but she'd been awake enough to appreciate the mouthwatering, pussy spasming view.

Lillian shook her head, admitting he was right; her thoughts about him jumped back and forth as much as his treatment of her. For two days, ever since she'd fled Brad's house, got in her car and just drove, she'd been operating on remote control. She still had no destination in mind for when she left here and didn't want to think ahead to the bleak future without Liana. Living for the moment was all she cared to do right now, and the sudden urge to have some fun with the good doctor took hold.

Squatting down, she scooped up a wad of snow and formed a snowball, intent on showing Mitchell she was perfectly capable of deciding how much rest or inactivity she could handle. She was bruised and sore, nothing she didn't have experience with even if this was the first time Brad had unleashed such uncontrolled anger on her and aimed for her ribs and face. She hoped the gash on his head she'd inflicted pained him as much as what she suffered.

Taking aim, she let loose with the snowball, wincing at the pull around her upper torso. The extra discomfort was worth it when Mitchell spun around in surprise and glared at her.

"Knock it off, Lillian," he growled as she scooped up another wad of snow in her gloved hands. "You're supposed to be resting."

"I don't need to rest. I slept twelve hours between yesterday and this morning." She shivered as he fisted his hands on those lean hips and his hazel eyes darkened to almost solid brown. She was learning to detect his mood by the color of his eyes and that look was becoming familiar, as was her heated response to his deep, demanding tone.

"I think I'm better qualified to know what you need to do. Now put that down and get back inside," he ordered.

Oh, no, neither that dictate nor her body's strange reaction was acceptable, leaving her only one way to retaliate. "*Tsk, tsk*, Doc, you're getting bossy again." Lobbing the snowball, she hit him in the chest. The disbelief on his face was comical until he came toward her with stealthy purpose.

Sparring with Mitchell helped keep her mind off her plight better than anything else thus far. Laughing, she held out a hand, as if that would hold him back. "You have to be nice, I'm hurt, remember?"

"You just said you were fine," he reminded her in a voice soft as silk, moving through the knee-high pileup much faster and easier than she.

Lillian backed away with a shiver, her pulse leaping as he closed the distance between them before she could reach the door. In her clumsy haste, she lost her footing and went down, the snow softening her fall but chilling her to the bone as the back of her bare head dampened. Mitchell came down on top of her, bracing on his arms, a small grin replacing the stern slash of his mouth.

"Serves you right for disobeying me."

Lillian's breath stalled and her heart thudded against her chest as Mitchell's face looming above her blurred into Brad's, his words hurling her back to the last time Brad's threats forced her to endure his possession. For a few seconds, the same sense of humiliation, throat-tightening despair and white-hot fury clouded her mind. Refusing to give in to the panicked distress threatening her composure, she snapped back as quickly as she'd tumbled down that rabbit hole, Mitchell's whiplash voice helping her to refocus on the present.

"*Lillian!*"

Getting to his feet, Mitchell throttled back his volatile reaction to seeing Lillian's face go chalk-white and her eyes glaze with such a look of torment he could feel her distress. She rallied as fast as she'd shaken him with the knowledge that bastard had done more than strike her. She started to get up and he held out his hand. "Give me your hand."

"I don't need help."

"Damn it." Grasping her arms, he lifted her up, his efforts earning him a glare out of those dark eyes. "Yes, you do, whether you want to admit it or not." As much as her intrusion on his privacy frustrated him, he once again found himself admiring her gumption as she shoved back whatever memory he'd triggered that had wiped the mirth off her face.

Lillian pulled away and he released her, his own thoughts as jumbled as hers appeared to be. Mitchell didn't want to involve himself in whatever trouble she was running from but couldn't deny the desire to see her face infused with pleasure just once before they went their separate ways. It wouldn't change the harm done to her, but it sure as hell would make him feel better, and her too for a short time.

"I think I'll listen to you and get back inside."

With some difficulty, he refrained from telling her to sit in front of the fire until her hair dried. "I'll be in shortly." He waited until the door closed behind her to retrieve his coat and gather up an armful of chopped wood.

Mitchell had been reminiscing about the long weekends he and Abbie had enjoyed at their mountain cabin back in Colorado when Lillian startled him with that first snowball. The unexpected cold *splat* jerked him back from the heated memory of restraining his naked wife to a tree one summer afternoon in the secluded copse of their private retreat and the way her soft cries would echo on the fresh mountain air. Lillian's amused defiance when he'd ordered her to stop and go back inside had shaken loose his ire, the impish look on her face and sparking in her eyes preferable to the desolation, pain or simmering anger she'd been portraying.

Too bad his attempt to playfully show her who held the upper hand had triggered a memory that wiped off her engaging smile. He craved five minutes with the man who had tormented her, the strangling tentacles of his rage on her behalf unlike anything he'd experienced before. The cases of abuse that had come through the trauma center in Denver had stirred his pity and anger, but Lillian's grit and determination in the wake of her trauma punched both those emotions up a notch. Considering that, he thought it was a good thing they would go their separate ways tomorrow.

Mitchell used his elbow to unlatch the door and shoved it open with his shoulder. Kicking it shut behind him, he turned with his load toward the fireplace and saw Lillian sitting on the hearth, the soft amber glow from the sizzling embers highlighting the dark burgundy of her shoulder-length hair. At least the stirring of lust he felt when she lifted her head and gave him a bland look was a familiar reaction he could accept much easier than what her expression lying under him in the snow had conjured up.

Dropping the logs except the bottom two into the bin, he said, "If you'll move aside for a minute, I'll stoke the fire."

"Sure. My hair's dry, so I don't need to sit this close anymore. Do you mind if I raid your food supply and come up with something for dinner? It would give me something to do."

"Knock yourself out, but I only stock the basics, some frozen hamburger and canned goods."

He listened to her rummaging as he got the fire up and going again and then spotted the notebook he gave her sitting on the end of the hearth. Picking it up, he flipped through it, gazing at the three pictures drawn with a talented hand. The woman in all three appeared to be Lillian until he looked closer at the details of her face. The nose was slightly off with a small bump, the eyes were the same oval shape but Lillian's lower lip was fuller than the woman in the pictures, and this woman's hair curled under her chin instead of hanging down her back.

Because of the resemblance, he assumed the drawing depicted a family member. "Who is this?" He held up the top sketch as she peered around from searching an upper cupboard.

Lillian's slender body went rigid, her jaw tightening and her eyes filling with sorrow and then narrowing to slits. He stayed patient while waiting for her to answer, which she did after several moments of tense silence between them.

"My twin sister. Does chili work for you?" She turned away from him and lifted down two cans of beans.

"Sounds good. You're an excellent artist. Will your supplies be okay sitting out there in these temperatures?"

"No. I'll have to replace my paints. I need a big pot."

Setting the tablet on the table, he walked over and pulled a large pan from under the sink and placed it on the burner before getting nosy again. "What happened to her?"

"She died," Lillian returned, her clipped voice conveying both grief and anger. "Unless you want to chop onion, leave me alone to get this going."

"I'll pass. That way you can blame your tears on the vegetable."

Lillian blinked away the watery sheen in her eyes, gritting her teeth to keep from railing at him and his inquisitiveness. She owed him for helping her, but not enough to give him more details about the circumstances leading up to Liana's passing. She didn't need anyone judging her for giving in to Brad's blackmail.

They settled into a companionable silence with him relaxing in the recliner with a book while she browned hamburger with onions and then stirred in the beans. As it simmered, she returned to the table to sketch another picture, this one of Mitchell with the glow of the blazing fire behind him. If she had her colored drawing pencils, she would shade the right side of his rugged face with a yellow tint. She eyed the mix of grey and black coloring of his hair and goatee, wondering about his age. The small lines fanning out from the corners of his eyes could be from squinting against the sun since she doubted they were laugh lines. She'd caught the same bleakness crossing his face she'd lived with since losing her twin but didn't care to delve into his personal issues any more than she wanted him inquiring about hers.

"What do you want to ask me, pet?" Mitchell looked up from

his book and nailed her with one of those probing stares that never failed to shake loose something inside her.

Ignoring the undesirable response, Lillian scowled. "Do you call me that just to annoy me?"

"Partly. Now, ask."

She couldn't fault him for being honest even if the continued use of the generic endearment grated on her nerves. "I was wondering about your age." Waving a hand toward his head, she said, "Your hair color on a woman would make her look older, but on men it's deceiving."

"I'm forty-two and the premature gray runs in my family."

Closing his book, he set it aside, pushed to his feet and stretched. Lillian admired his lean height, guessing he stood around six-four as she recalled what he looked like naked, his impressive, ripcord muscles and deceptive strength. Her blood flow heated, forcing her gaze away before he noticed her staring. The only explanation for her continued, strong responses must be stress, but regardless, she wasn't in the market for another relationship. Not even a strictly physical one. She shut the notebook and went to dish out the chili thinking tomorrow and the snowplows couldn't come soon enough.

Like last night, Lillian donned his shirt and climbed into bed hours before Mitchell, staring into the fire until the heat and wavering flames lulled her to sleep. But unlike the previous night, tonight she wasn't weighed down with exhaustion to keep the bad dreams at bay. Visions of happy times with her sister kept getting jumbled with the weeks she'd lived on edge under Brad's roof.

"Come on, sis. You can do it." Lillian held her hand down from where she sat perched on the limb of the large oak tree in their front yard. "But hurry, before Mom sees us and makes us do chores."

"I don't know why I let you talk me into these things, Lil." Liana grabbed her hand and swung up onto the branch next to her just as their mother popped her head out the back door and called for them.

They both giggled, refusing to answer until they were threatened with getting grounded for a month.

"I love you, but I'm not missing the eighth-grade dance just to get out of cleaning my room." Liana delivered a playful punch to her arm and then jumped to the ground.

Lillian groaned, clutched her arm and rolled over as Brad's cold voice replaced her sister's happy lilt.

Gripping her upper arm as she entered the house, Brad swung her about with an angry glare. "Where the fuck have you been?"

Her arm throbbed and Lillian pictured the new bruise already forming. Gritting her teeth, she ground out, "I told you I had an art class this evening."

Yanking her against him, his eyes bored into hers. "You better not be lying. One injection and Liana will suffer." Releasing her arm, he delivered a punch to her stomach that doubled her over on a gasp. "Now come upstairs and make it up to me." He hauled her up the stairs, Lillian cringing at the thought of him touching her again.

She let her mind go blank as he stripped her, following his demands with feigned enthusiasm. He never hurt her in bed. On the contrary, he whispered words of apology, his touch gentle, his praise of her over the top. She went along, nodded her forgiveness and accepted his thrusts, all the while vowing revenge one day…

With a quiet sob, Lillian slid out of the bed before she woke Mitchell. The extra warmth from the simmering embers beckoned and she padded across the wood planking to stand on the braided rug before the low, crackling flames. Her heart pounded and her body quaked from the conflicting emotions of sadness and fury, making her wonder which would eventually overtake the other. She'd always been the instigator of trouble and daring between her and Liana, her little stunts landing them in hot water nine times out of ten. She was used to accepting the blame and figured that was why she kept faulting herself for something neither of them could have seen coming. Her shame stemmed from being unable to find a way to defy Brad's threats and keep

Liana safe, and she needed to learn to live with her degrading compliance to his possession and painful punches.

"Are you okay?"

Lillian stiffened, anger rising to the surface with Mitchell's intrusion. "I'm fine. Sorry I woke you," she replied without turning around. Between sorrow pricking her eyes from missing Liana and bile lodged in her throat from recalling the distaste of Brad's touch, she didn't trust herself to remain bottled up if she faced him.

Mitchell fisted his hands to keep from reaching for Lillian. Her soft moan of distress had woken him from a light sleep and he'd opened his eyes to see her walking to the fireplace. His shirt hung to her mid-thighs, leaving those long, slender legs bare. Need poured off her rigid body in waves as she looked down at the small, residual glow. For what, he didn't know and shouldn't care. So why was he standing behind her now, listening to her lie when she said she was fine? He swore he possessed no desire to get involved with her troubles, but the sob wrenched from her throat that had roused him shredded that resolve, the quiver in her voice just now tugging at his compassion.

"Now, that's a lie, pet," he admonished, injecting a note of steel in his tone. He hated to ask but needed to know. "Were you raped?"

She whirled on him so fast, he took a step back, those purple eyes blazing with hate and a hint of shame, her face red, either from the heat or anger, he couldn't tell which. "No. I went to his bed willingly every time he bruised me. And if you think that makes me a pathetic moron, too stupid to live, I don't give a damn." Lillian poked a finger at his bare chest, the jab landing right between his pecs. "Quit calling me pet. I don't like it."

Mitchell thanked his considerable control as he moved forward again, close enough his flannel shirt she wore brushed his abdomen. "I don't think anything because that's not the whole truth. There are all kinds of ways to coerce an unwilling woman. If you don't want to tell me, fine by me. Since we will be parting ways tomorrow, you won't have to hear me calling you pet again, which is good because I don't take orders, I give them."

Her jaw tightened as she gave one jerky nod and spun around again, but not before he caught the same flash of despair in her eyes he'd glimpsed several times before, the same despondency that still pulled him down when he thought of Abbie.

"Then there's nothing else to say, is there?" The slight catch in Lillian's whisper belied her stiff stance of peevish anger.

No matter how much he did not want to involve himself, he couldn't leave her hurting. Like he said, they would be going their separate ways within hours. What could it hurt if he gave her a better memory to think about when the bad ones intruded? It would sure help ease his conscience if he could send her on her way knowing he'd done what he could to help her cope with her demons.

"How long has your sister been gone?"

She sucked in a breath and whispered, "Come morning, five days."

Mitchell swore, sympathizing with her. The acute pain of his own loss had abated to a dull ache, but those first days of shocked grief were still too easy to recall. Before he could change his mind, he rested his hands on her shoulders and rubbed the tenseness out of them until she released her pent-up breath on a sigh. Then he slid his hands down her arms, circled her wrists and lifted her hands to the wooden mantel just above her head.

Leaning his head down sideways, he rested his lips against her ear. "You've trusted me for two days. Trust me a little longer and leave your hands there until I give you permission to lower them."

Her back muscles went taut and this time, her whisper trembled. "Why? What are you going to do?"

"Make you forget the bad for a short time. Give you a new, better memory to leave here with. Trust me to do that."

Mitchell kept his hands over hers and called on his patience as Lillian took her time answering. When she did, the relief and pleasure her reply sent rushing through him would bear deeper scrutiny later, much later.

"Okay, yes, I'll do that."

Chapter 4

Lillian had washed out her bra and panties and left them drying in the bathroom before turning in, and now braced herself as Mitchell reached around her and unbuttoned the shirt, wondering what the heck she was doing. She was done taking orders from men, wasn't she? He hadn't asked for her trust, he'd insisted on it. The seductive promise interlaced with the deep voiced command had tugged at something inside her, an ache for what he was promising, and prompted her to agree just to see where this would go.

She sucked in a deep breath as the shirt fell open and the warmth from the fireplace added to the instant heat of his nails scraping across her nipples. How long had it been since she'd allowed herself to enjoy a man's touch? Months, she figured, and hadn't cared until now. One touch from Mitchell and she craved more.

"Very good, Lillian. I like your body, so soft," he cupped her breasts, "and dainty." Her small fleshy mounds filled the palm of his hands. "And here," he brushed her nipples with his thumbs, "so hard and quick to respond. You will tell me if I do anything that triggers a bad memory or response."

"Bossy," she huffed on an exasperated laugh. "Have I mentioned I don't like bossy men?"

"A time or two." Releasing her breasts, he gathered the sides of the shirt and pulled them back, doing some twists and tucks until the wadded material rested in a knot against her lower back.

A shiver raced down Lillian's spine as his fingers trailed across her exposed buttocks, drawing goosebumps and a new awareness of that part of her body. And then he slapped her cheek, nothing more than the bounce of his hand on her flesh, the minor sting quickly changing to a warm throb. She wanted to question him but didn't trust her voice not to betray the odd quiver of embarrassing arousal that smack produced. Another light tap fell on her other buttock and she held her breath against the same response.

"Mitchell," she gasped as he slid one hand down between her cheeks, grazing her private rear orifice while cupping his other hand between her legs from the front.

"You surprise me, in a good way, pet. I thought I would have to coax a response from you, and yet you're already damp." He pressed both hands against her sensitive flesh, the pressure drawing more of her cream.

Shaken in more ways than one, she grumbled, "I thought I wouldn't have to hear you call me pet again."

"I slipped. I'll make it up to you." Mitchell delivered another teasing swat to her vulnerable backside followed by a slow glide of one finger along her pussy seam, a tickle that distracted from the slight sting.

Lillian had never experienced such focused foreplay or such attention to her butt. She didn't know if she liked it so much because she needed the distraction from the emotional upheaval of the past six weeks or because it had been so long since she'd enjoyed the pleasures of a man's touch that she would take anything she could get. She wanted to come back with a sharp retort, but he took that moment to part her labia and work two fingers into her sheath, taking his time to graze along sensitive nerve endings begging for attention.

"Yes," she groaned as he pulled back to circle her clit with one finger.

"No bad moments?" Mitchell asked, pulling out of her to tease her pussy lips with his damp fingers.

She shook her head, aching for more. "No, I'm fine."

"You'll set yourself up for additional heartache if someone asks if you're okay and you toss out that standard comeback when it's not true," he warned in a silky whisper, his lips brushing her earlobe.

She blew out a frustrated breath as goosebumps popped up along her neck and arms. "But it is true now, and now is all that matters." Pushing her hips back, she pled, "Please don't make me wait."

"Damn if you're not hard to resist, and I wouldn't admit that to just anyone."

Any other time and place, that confession would stroke her ego, but the need to escape from the desolation that had consumed her for so long took precedence. Mitchell thrust back up inside her and Lillian exhaled on a relieved breath before he robbed her of it by finger-fucking her with deep, well-aimed strokes. He slid the hand nestled between her buttocks around her waist and up to her breasts to squeeze one round globe.

Pleasure engulfed her body as he plucked at a nipple and her clit, the little squeezes zapping the tender buds with arousing heat. She tightened her hands on the edge of the mantel, grateful now for his order to keep them there. Bracing her locked arms aided in keeping her anchored, both physically and mentally, while she fought against giving in to her wobbly legs and degrading memories.

"Let go if you're ready, Lillian. I'm right here to catch you."

The promise, given in that toe-curling guttural tone, accompanied the steady milking of her swollen bundle of nerves. She quaked as arousal spiked out of control, the first pop of pleasure replacing the pain of her last encounter, the shock to her battered system wrenching a cry from her throat. A surge of pure delight rushed through her body as she bucked against his marauding hand and pushed against his hold on her breast. For a few blissful moments, she was swept away on a tidal wave of pleasure that drenched her body and drowned her sorrow.

"Again," he ordered while she was still relishing the ebbing smaller contractions of her orgasm. He went deep again, so deep, so fast and hard, the plunge brought her up on her toes.

"I don't think I can," she moaned, but that didn't stop her from arching back and accepting another twist of his wrist as he withdrew and then returned to continue to stoke the damp heat in her quivering pussy.

"Yes, you can," he insisted, and then set about proving it as he alternated thrusting with hard pressure against her clit and moved back and forth between her nipples, pinching, rolling and caressing the throbbing tips.

"Oh, God." Drenched in heated pleasure, Lillian embraced the sweeping wave of another climax, shaken by how fast his hands produced another one, longing for the pleasure to continue as she descended from the exultant high. Once it stopped completely, reality would rear its ugly head and she wanted to stave off facing her loss again for as long as possible. "Mitchell, don't stop," she pleaded without looking back at him, too mortified by the depth of her uncharacteristic degeneracy.

Mitchell searched for his control as Lillian arched into his hands, her tortured plea cutting through his stoic resistance to sinking his cock between her silken folds. Her cum soaked his fingers, her slick walls still spasming around them as he soothed the pinches to her nipples with light caresses. The firelight bathed her pale, bowed body in a burnt orange glow, emphasizing the stark whiteness of her skin and the colored bruising around her ribs. He could see the side view of the soft fullness of her small breasts and feel the contrasting stiffness of the turgid tips against his fingertips.

She presented a temptation he found hard to resist, more so after she'd willingly kept her hands where he had positioned them. He doubted a hidden core of submissiveness compelled her to obey that order; she hadn't portrayed a hint of compliancy since he found her until now, so there must be another reason she hadn't slipped from the pose.

"I planned to spend the week alone, so I don't have a condom." With slow deliberation, he pulled out of her pussy, her low groan of disappointment mirroring what he felt.

"I'm on the pill but haven't taken them in two days since they're still packed in my car." She swiveled her head, her cascade of auburn hair swinging over her upper arm as she slowly lowered her hands.

Mitchell loosened the knotted shirt, the forlornness in her eyes getting to him before she masked it with cool acceptance. He had never fucked bareback, not with anyone except Abbie. He enjoyed the wet clasp of a woman's tight muscles massaging his bare flesh as much as any guy, but it was an intimacy he'd only shared with his wife. So why the prickle of regret for turning Lillian down now?

The shirt fell down to her sides and she turned around, standing before him with unabashed concern as he raked his eyes over her breasts and down her body. The neatly trimmed auburn curls between her legs offered just a peek at the still puffy folds he'd traced with his fingers, her frontal nakedness as enticing as her soft buttocks and long legs.

Hoping to lighten the sudden tense silence, he said, "Maybe we can take this further next time. You should try to get some more sleep."

Without rising to the bait or saying anything else, Lillian walked around him, went into the bathroom for a few minutes and then got back into bed. Mitchell caught a glimpse of the edge of her pink panties and figured she needed to don as much armor against him and what he'd given her as she could. Given how badly he wanted to take that short scene further, or devise another one, it was a good thing they would go their separate ways later today. He wasn't interested in another relationship, and coming off an abused one, he doubted she was either. Besides, vanilla and BDSM don't mix well, regardless of his success in pulling her mind off her troubles for a short time by giving her a taste of the control he liked to exert during sex.

The rescue crew couldn't come soon enough, Mitchell thought as he settled in the recliner, shut his eyes and the first thing to pop up was Lillian's flushed face, dark eyes and the tight clutch of her damp muscles around his fingers.

"Thanks, Grayson. We'll head over." Mitchell clicked off the satellite phone and nodded at Lillian. "They've about got you dug out so I'll walk you back."

For the first time since waking a few hours ago, Lillian's tense muscles relaxed. She was more than ready to get going and put as much distance between her host and herself as she could. With her body still humming from his touch and her dreams of him smacking her butt even harder followed by driving his cock into her body over and over still way too vivid in her head, she needed alone time to get herself under control. "Great. I'll get my coat."

Mitchell arched a brow as he handed her her coat and reached for his. "I see you're as happy about leaving as I am about getting my place back to myself."

Lillian paused in pulling on her gloves. "It's not that I'm not grateful. But last night, well," she struggled for what to say and he didn't offer to help. Jerking on her glove, her frustration came through as she grumbled, "It was just the tense circumstances, not like either one of us wants a repeat."

"No, we definitely wouldn't want that," he murmured, the look on his face indiscernible. "Let's go."

He took her hand and didn't let go as they left the warmth of the cabin and traversed through the knee-high snow toward the woods separating them from the road. Halfway through the trees, they spotted the blinking yellow lights on a large snowplow truck and the swirling blue strobe of the county sheriff's cruiser.

Mitchell squeezed her hand and gazed down at her, frowning as those observant eyes roamed over her still bruised face. "You need to stop at a clinic and get checked again in a few days, just to ensure your ribs are healing. I hope you're planning on staying as far away from whoever hurt you as possible."

Lillian nodded, glad he hadn't pestered her for details these past few days. "Don't worry, we're done for good." With Liana gone, there was nothing left for Brad to blackmail her with.

"Good to know." He tugged her forward, lifting a hand in a wave and Lillian saw a tall man wearing a Stetson, a toothpick nestled in the corner of his mouth return the greeting.

It wasn't until they crossed the now packed-down, snow encrusted road and were within a few feet of the man that she noticed the law enforcement stenciling on his leather jacket. Beneath the lowered brim of his hat, the sheriff's gray/green gaze turned flinty as he zeroed in on her bruised face. He pinned those anger swirling eyes on Mitchell so fast, Lillian shifted toward her host in an unconscious show of support.

"Explain," the sheriff demanded, his tone short and clipped.

Mitchell shrugged. "She came that way. I've checked her over."

Irritated with the show of machoism, she yanked her arm out of Mitchell's hold and ground out, "She's right here and can answer for herself."

With a wry twist of his lips, Mitchell drawled, "Sheriff Grayson Monroe, this is Lillian…" He paused and lifted a brow.

For the first time in as long as she could remember, Lillian grew warm from embarrassment as Grayson's stern look changed to one of amusement. It was mortifying to realize she'd just spent over two days with a man and an hour last night with his hands all over her naked body, his fingers deep inside her, and they knew very little about each other. She hadn't even given him her last name. She'd never indulged in casual sex and still couldn't fathom what had gotten into her last night. The temptation to accept the temporary diversion from her grief he'd offered in his deep, seductive voice had been impossible to resist.

"Gillespie," she said, holding out her hand to the sheriff as the plow truck driver joined them.

Grayson took her hand, holding onto to her as he asked, "Ma'am. Is the person responsible for those bruises from around here?"

The other man scowled as he noticed her face. "No. I left him in Utah." Turning to the truck driver, she asked, "Am I good to go?"

"'Fraid not, ma'am. I've got you dug out, but you've got a broken axle. I've called the shop in Willow Springs and Mort's son, Andy is on his way with the tow truck. Don't you worry none." The burly man reached over and squeezed her shoulder. "Mort'll get you up and running in no time."

Lillian's shoulders slumped. She'd been hoping to get back on the road again. She wasn't far enough away from her memories to suit her yet. "How long will it take, do you think?"

The sheriff nudged his hat back and blew out a white puff of breath. "I know he's backed up with this weather causing several mishaps. You can get your things out of your car and I'll take you to the motel, then you can give Mort a call."

"Come on, I'll help you," Mitchell offered.

At least she wouldn't be stuck at his cabin any longer, she mused as the three of them tromped to her car. With the men insisting they could get everything, including her artwork and supplies, she was left to stand aside and watch them transfer her belongings to the back of the SUV cruiser. It would be good to change clothes and lose herself in painting again, provided her oils were still usable after being frozen. At least being stranded this time around she would have something to pass the time besides trying to figure out how Dr. Mitchell Hoffstetter could arouse her to such a degree when she found him so bossy and irritating.

Taking a deep breath as the last of her things were loaded in the cruiser, she turned to Mitchell with her hand out, which seemed lame after the orgasms he'd given her just a few hours earlier. "Thank you for everything. I owe you."

"Maybe I'll collect if you're in town long enough. If you're still there when I return at the end of the week, come by the clinic next Monday. It wouldn't hurt to get those ribs x-rayed."

Lillian nodded with no intention of looking him up.

Salt Lake City

"I don't fucking understand you." Bryan McCabe took a long draw on his cigarette, glaring at his much younger brother as anger toward the woman who had gone ballistic on Brad warred with concern over his little brother's blurred vision and dizzy spells. If Brad's health was bad enough to keep him home from the hospital for a third day in a row, then it was time for him to get himself checked by another physician other than himself. "You need to let me drive you to the hospital and then go after that bitch. It's not right to let her get away with ambushing and assaulting you." He still couldn't believe the polite, rather meek woman he'd met one time had turned on Brad in a fit of jealousy before taking off, but Brad's injury was real, and potentially debilitating if he continued to be so stubborn about getting checked.

"I said no and put out that damn cigarette." Brad leaned his head back on the sofa and closed his eyes. "She's not a threat to me. The only reason she got in this one good whack," he waved a hand at his bandaged forehead, "was because I wasn't prepared for her to go at me like that. I should have let her down easier when I said I wanted her to move out. Her possessiveness was just one of the things that had grown tiresome about our relationship."

That wasn't surprising, Bryan thought, inhaling another deep, nicotine rush. Brad had a way about him that drew women. Between his elevated status as one of the top surgeons in the city and reputation as a much sought-after eligible bachelor, it was no wonder Lillian Gillespie had fallen hard and fast for his brother. But that was no excuse for laying into him, catching him unaware as he had returned home after asking her to pack up and leave.

"I don't give a shit about her hurt feelings. She committed a crime, Brad, and I want her charged." Bryan gave in to Brad's pointed glare and stubbed out the offending smoke in a dish his brother left on the end table just for him. Folding his arms, he leaned against the fireplace mantle in front of the sofa. His only sibling and family deserved this big, fancy house and all the adulation heaped upon him for the lives he saved. Of the two of them, he was the smartest and the most driven. There was a ten-year gap in their ages, and after their single mother had passed away when Brad was eleven, Bryan had willingly moved back into their mother's house to finish raising him. From the first time school bullies had picked on Brad, he had looked out for him, stood up for him and made it a point to always be there when he needed him.

In Bryan's opinion, little brother needed his interference in this matter, whether he wanted to admit it or not. As a cop, he was privy to resources that would provide him with the means to charge Lillian. All he had to do was track her down.

"Again, no, now let it go. I don't want to see her hurt." Brad opened his eyes and returned Bryan's glare. "Come on, bro. I've got a mild concussion. Trust me, I would know if it was anything worse than that. She got in a lucky wallop and I didn't dodge fast enough. Let it go. I already have," he insisted.

Pushing away from the fireplace, he dropped his arms with a scowl. "I will, for now, but if you're not up and about like normal soon, I'll revisit the idea of arresting her sorry ass." Pivoting, he stalked across the gleaming marbled floor and snatched his coat off a coat tree in the entry. Calling back, he said, "I'll be back after my shift."

Brad winced as his brother slammed the front door behind him. Damn Bryan's overprotectiveness and Lillian's conniving. He had gone cold when she'd tossed out that shocking revelation of having documented her bruises. He knew exactly where to hit, and how hard to deliver the most painful impact without causing internal damage. Until he'd come home and found her packed up and ready to walk out of his life again, he'd been careful not to leave bruises where anyone could see them. Given the fear he'd instilled in her regarding her precious, comatose sister, he never doubted she would rat him out to anyone.

Bryan wouldn't believe her without proof, he was too busy playing the saintly big brother to see what was right in front of him. Brad's high intellect put him in the category of god status, and damned if he didn't like it there. No woman had ever left him; he was always the one to end things. He'd been shocked when Lillian had broken off with him the first time they were together, and fucking pissed since he'd already decided she would make the perfect trophy wife. As an artist, he'd never seen better and with his connections, he could have taken her career higher.

He chuckled now, thinking about how the perfect opportunity to get her back had landed in his lap with Liana's aneurysm. It wouldn't have bothered him in the least to cause that girl untold suffering if Lillian had tested his blackmail threats since Liana's dislike of him had contributed to Lillian ending their relationship the first time. He hadn't counted on the stupid bitch up and dying, at least not that soon.

"Well, it doesn't matter now," he muttered, pushing to his feet. The room spun in circles, fast enough to force him to sit back down and put his head between his knees. Fuck but he would give anything to make her pay for laying him so low. Too bad those pictures she'd taken ensured he wouldn't take his revenge on her. No woman was worth losing his stellar reputation or status in the city over.

He just hoped he got over this concussion soon and that Bryan would cool down and forget about going after her.

Lillian sipped the piping hot coffee the motel manager had delivered first thing that morning, the same as yesterday and the day before. She'd already devoured the Danish he'd added this time. She sighed, gazing at the trash filled with the paints that were too lumpy to keep, which was most of them. They'd thawed out after twenty-four hours but only a few were still usable. Frustrated at the loss and with being holed up in the small town of Willow Springs' only motel for three days, she looked out the window at the fields of solid white. There was no denying the pristine view of distant, snow-capped mountains and the trees that stayed green year-round with icicles hanging off their limbs. So much open space; what the heck do people do out here?

She'd ventured out on foot yesterday for a walk and to snap a few pictures to paint from. The roads were cleared and the downtown district wasn't far off, but the biting cold had deterred her from making the trek toward the clump of buildings. Too bad nothing had worked to keep her mind from replaying that late night, foolish scene with her less-than-welcoming cabin host. Doc Mitchell hadn't been rude or made her unplanned stay uncomfortable. On the contrary, he had made her as comfortable as he could even though he hadn't disguised his annoyance with having his solitary sojourn interrupted. She appreciated his help but his bossiness irritated her. She was grateful for the free medical check and advice that had given her peace of mind but berating her for pushing herself had rubbed her the wrong way. Grief accounted for her irresponsibility in neglecting to get her injuries checked, but she'd believed, and was right, they weren't life-threatening.

And what did she care about the relief in the good doctor's hazel eyes when the sheriff had hustled her into his cruiser and Mitchell waved goodbye? Just because the man had taken her to exalted heights of ecstasy she'd never achieved before, or even thought possible, was no reason for his rugged face to keep popping up or for her to continue recalling how her nipples would peak from the deep rumble of his commanding voice.

I need to get away from here, that's all. Yes, that was all there was to the frustration of sitting here idly daydreaming about a man she knew little about except his touch could set her off like a firecracker. Stress, grief and anger were powerful motivators for succumbing to a virtual stranger she wasn't sure she even liked, but that was over and she was more than ready to put him and this place behind her.

The problem was, where to next? And, how far would she have to travel to escape the painful memories she'd left behind? Lillian missed her sister with a deep-rooted ache. She'd thought the six weeks Liana had lain in a coma had prepared Lillian for never hearing her voice again, but she'd thought wrong. She still found herself reaching for the phone to make their daily call. They'd been as close as twins could be yet had respected each other's need for space and forging their own path in life.

Liana hadn't hesitated in supporting Lillian's initial break with Brad; her sister had never warmed up to him. Thank God Liana had never gotten wind of how crazy possessive he was. At least her comatose state spared her the knowledge of his depraved blackmail and the degrading lengths Lillian had been willing to accept to spare her pain.

A rap on the door roused her from her melancholy. The motel manager called out, "It's Bob from the front desk, Ms. Gillespie."

Opening the door, Lillian handed the white-haired man her empty coffee cup and plate. "Thank you so much."

"No problem. I'm leaving in about fifteen minutes, if you'd like to get out a spell I can give you a lift to our business square.

There are some small shops, a tea café that is popular, the diner and the library, all within easy walking around. I figured you might be getting cabin fever, holed up in here for so long."

"I'd love that." Anything to take her mind off missing her sister. Bob always eyed her fading bruises with a tight look of disapproval, his concern both unsettling and warming. A bit like her response to Mitchell's same reaction upon first gazing at her face. "Just let me grab my coat and I'll head over to the office."

He nodded. "See you in a few minutes. Don't forget gloves, and a hat if you have one."

The fatherly advice was unnecessary, but nonetheless, appreciated. With her whole family now gone, Lillian embraced the older man's solicitude. She didn't have a hat but would be warm enough in her thigh-length, lined coat and gloves. Enduring a little cold was worth it for the chance at something to do. Funny, she mused as she trekked toward the idling car in front of the motel office, the boredom and close confines of staying in the doc's cabin hadn't gotten under her skin like these past days in the motel had. At least she would be spared an awkward moment of meeting up with Mitchell again today since he was enjoying his solitude now she was out of his hair.

Bob pulled in front of the Willow Springs library, housed in a renovated, hundred-year-old building. The quaint town square was something out of a history book; only the touches of modern-day advances such as the streetlamps and center fountain ensured first-time visitors they hadn't stepped back in time. The city offices and sheriff's precinct were in the two-story, all brick building next to the library, and she recalled the sexy, toothpick chewing lawman whose penetrating looks had given her shivers of awareness that he was not a man to cross. She didn't fear him, in fact, didn't fear any man, not even Brad at his worst. But, like Mitchell, Grayson Monroe had commanded her attention with just a look and a few words, something she wasn't used to.

"You tell Willa I dropped you off. She'll help you find what you like and can point you in the right direction of any shops you might want to visit. I have your number. I'll check with you in a little while, see if you need a lift back."

"That's nice of you, but I don't want to put you out. It's not that far of a walk." She couldn't imagine any other motel manager going to such lengths for a guest.

"On a nice day, it's doable, but not in the winter. I'm already in town. It's no imposition."

"Then thank you."

Even though there were several books on her reader Lillian hadn't gotten to yet, she liked the idea of killing time by searching for a title or two in paperback. The building even smelled old, she reflected as she stepped inside and spotted the eighty-something librarian behind the check-out counter. Always before, she had Liana to recommend books and compare their likes and dislikes with. It was her sister who turned Lillian into an avid reader, and as she walked toward the counter, her stomach cramped from another painful reminder of her loss.

"Good morning. Are you all right, dear?" The older woman shuffled toward her with a frown of concern.

"Yes, I'm fine," Lillian rushed to assure her as a short brunette wearing wide, dark-framed glasses approached the desk carrying several books. She waved an airy hand around her face, remembering the now sickly shades of yellow and green her bruises had faded into. "This mishap occurred several days ago. I'm only in town a few more days while my car's getting fixed. Would a temporary library card be possible?"

The brunette set her books down and swiveled to look at Lillian with a surprised expression that switched to curiosity. "You must be Doc's stranded guest. Hi, I'm Avery Monroe, the sheriff's wife." She held out a hand and her coat fell open to reveal a small baby bump.

"That would be me, Lillian Gillespie." She took her hand wishing she possessed a fraction of the other woman's curves.

"You *have* to join me at the tea shop after you get your books and tell us about having our good doctor all to yourself for almost three days. We're dying of curiosity." Avery's eyes sparkled and her teasing grin was contagious.

Small town living, don't ya just love it? Lillian thought back to the intense heat of that hour by the fireplace, not all of it coming from the flames crackling in front of her naked body. "Word travels fast around here, doesn't it? I hate to burst your bubble, but there's not much to tell. Mitchell wasn't too happy about having me there, but we both made the best of it." It wasn't as if she could tell a stranger something so private. It would likely shock Avery to hear how Lillian had obeyed his commands without much thought or hesitation. Heck, just thinking about her easy capitulation was a jolting reminder of how desperate she'd been for anything that would take her mind off facing the rest of her life without her twin and best friend at her side.

"Avery, why don't you show Lillian where to find the genres she's interested in. I'm Willa, dear, and yes, I'll have a temporary card ready for you when you've made your selections," the librarian said, handing her an information sheet to fill out.

"Sure, I'd love to. It's always fun to browse with someone who still enjoys reading print books." As soon as the two of them moved away from the counter, Avery whispered, "Please tell me there was more to your stay in the woods than that."

Seeing no polite way to refuse, Lillian pasted on a smile. The other woman's enthusiasm for gossip reminded her of Liana and how her sibling thrived on involving herself in her author's lives. "Sorry. He was a congenial host, well, except for his penchant for bossiness. The man never asked, just demanded."

Avery chuckled as she led Lillian toward the suspense section. "I know what you mean. My husband is the same way."

"And you don't mind?"

She shrugged. "Sometimes, but he has a way of making it worth not arguing too much."

"Huh. Well, no offense, but great sex still isn't worth putting up with overbearing bossiness."

"No, but awesome sex is, and besides, Grayson only turns really demanding and firm when he's concerned for me over something. That's nice, to know he cares so much. I never had that before him. Have you read this?" Avery pulled out a mystery thriller. "It's very good and has a surprise ending."

"I love surprise endings." Lillian took the book, envying the other woman's happiness and speculating about whether the perks from a committed, close relationship were worth putting up with a domineering man on occasion.

"Stick around here long enough and you might get one of your own, like me. So, what do you say?" Avery asked as they strode back to the counter "Do you have time for a cup of tea with me?"

I have nothing else to do, nowhere to go and no one else. And wasn't that the sad truth? "I'd love to. Thank you."

Chapter 5

The tea shop reminded Lillian of the coffee bar she often visited back home with its small dining area and long glass-enclosed counter showcasing sweets to go with the list of teas and coffees. She followed Avery to one of the round tables with wrought iron legs and matching chairs as the woman behind the counter glanced up with a welcoming smile.

"Hey, girlfriend. You're early, but that's fine by me. It's been slow this morning." Coming around the counter, the rich hue of her mink brown hair grazed her shoulders as she eyed Lillian out of light brown eyes. When she reached the table, she didn't shy away from eying her bruises with a wince. "Please don't say you ran into a wall."

Lillian chuckled. She liked her open candor. "Funny, that's almost the same thing Mitchell said. The man who did this is history and no longer a threat."

"Well, that's good to know." She thrust out a hand. "Mitchell, huh? You must be his rescued guest. I'm Nan."

She shook Nan's hand, wondering at all the interest in the local doctor's personal life. He was hot, yes, but given both women wore sparkling wedding rings, she doubted they were pining for male companionship. "I'm Lillian, and I'm not Mitchell's anything and prefer to keep it that way."

"Do tell but let me get you something first. I recommend the cherry green tea or sweet blackberry black tea to go with a cinnamon scone." Flicking Avery a look, she said, "Only green for you. The last time I caved and gave you the loaded coffee you wanted, Master Grayson reamed me good for abetting you in sneaking caffeine."

"That's not as bad as what he did to me." Avery sent Lillian a quick look and blushed before rolling her eyes and nudging her glasses back up. "We were just discussing bossy men and I told Lillian I don't mind it when my husband goes all caveman on me, but *sheesh*, his overprotectiveness has gone off the charts since I got pregnant."

One word stood out from Nan's remarks and drew on Lillian's curiosity. "Master? Is that a joke or nickname?"

"Definitely no joke. Our husbands like sexual control, along with protective streaks that can get annoying." Nan cocked her head. "Master Mitchell is good friends with them. I'm surprised you didn't pick up on it, staying in such close quarters for almost three days. It's not as if any of them shed their private personas completely to don a different attitude when not at their club."

"Huh, so that's where the bossiness comes from." Knowing the doctor was into the kinks of BDSM explained a lot, but not the ease with which she had accepted his commands. Lillian most definitely wasn't interested in letting a man dictate to her ever again, not even for rewarding sex. Needing to change the subject, she said, "The cherry green sounds good."

"Okay, make it two," Avery added then turned to Lillian. "I hope we didn't make you uncomfortable."

Lillian shook her head. "No, not at all. In fact, you're braver than I am. I've met your husband and don't think I'd go against his wishes."

A smile brightened Avery's face. "His bark is worse than his bite. Well," she shifted on the seat with an exaggerated grimace and sparkle in her caramel eyes. "Most of the time anyway."

Lillian would not ask. Just that slight movement hinted at where the sheriff had delivered his punishment and reminded her of the light swats Mitchell introduced her to. She hadn't minded those; in fact, she'd found the taps stimulating. A small souvenir to take with her when she got back on the road again in a few days.

"What are your plans while you're here?" Nan asked as she set a tray down with their tea and scones.

"I haven't made any except to find the arts and crafts shop the motel manager mentioned. I don't know how much longer it'll take for my car, but it should only be a few days." She blew on the hot beverage and took a sip, the steaming tea tasting good and easing her chills. Winter was not the best time to travel north.

"That'd be Maisie's over on Second Street. I'll give you a lift when you're done, if you want," Avery offered.

"Thanks, but I don't want to put you out. I'm sure I can find it, and Bob, from the motel, already offered to come back and pick me up."

"It's on my way, so it's no trouble. There's an accounting office on Second I've got an appointment at to check a downed computer."

"Okay, then thanks. It's quiet in here. Is that because of the snow?"

"Nah, weather rarely keeps anyone home around here," Nan replied. "It's always slow after the morning coffee rush. Most weeks, our friends, Sydney and Tamara join us on Wednesdays, but they're both in the final weeks of their third trimester and sticking close to home."

Lillian arched a brow as she swallowed a bite of pastry. "Is there something in the water I need to worry about?"

"Not unless you got closer to our good doctor than you said. There's just as many of us who aren't in a hurry to join them, even if Dan keeps hinting about the two of us not getting any younger," Nan returned.

"Speaking of your husband." Avery nodded toward the door as the bell above it jingled and a tall blond man wearing a dark brown Stetson, leather coat and cowboy boots sauntered in.

Nan stood with a beaming smile and Lillian experienced a tight clutch in her abdomen as her husband focused his dark eyes on her. Ignoring his audience, he cupped her nape and drew his wife's head up for a deep kiss that made Lillian question the enjoyment of her every lip lock. By the time he released Nan with a playful smack on her butt and nudged his hat back, she was the one squirming in her seat. Smiling, he said, "Good morning, ladies. You must be Mitchell's rescue. Dan Shylock."

"Again, I'm not the doctor's anything. Nice to meet you. I'm Lillian." Lillian shook his hand, bemused by how fast and far word had spread of the short time she'd spent snowed in with their resident physician.

"If you say so, Lillian." He turned back to Nan who had poured him a to-go cup. "Thank you. I've got to be in court this afternoon, wait for me and we'll go home together." He pinched Nan's chin. "I'm sure you can find something to amuse you until I get back from Billings."

"I'm sure I can," Nan drawled. "See you this evening."

"He is so hot." Avery fanned herself and Lillian had to agree as they watched him stroll out. There was something about the way the two of them looked at each other that prompted her to tighten her legs to still her quivering pussy.

Uncomfortable with her response, Lillian retorted without thinking, "He's as bossy as Mitchell," and then lifted stricken eyes up to Nan. "I'm sorry. That sounded rude."

Nan laughed. "No it didn't, it sounded honest. And accurate, he is bossy. I don't mind at the club, in fact, I love giving him control there. I didn't argue with him just now because I know he worries about me driving after dark when the roads are so much worse. You learn to pick your battles when you're married to a dominant man. Since I'll still be around this evening, how about dinner at Dale's Diner on the corner?"

Lillian marveled at the way both women welcomed her without hesitation, offering their time and company without pause to a stranger. Maybe they were curious about what went on with her and Mitchell, or maybe they were just nice people. Either way, their friendly overtures this morning meant a lot. "Can I give you my number and let you know after I get back to the motel? To be honest, I may not want to get out in the cold again."

"Can't blame you. Sure. I'll call when I'm ready to close up. Avery, I'll see you Saturday. You two take your time. I've got to get ready for the noon crowd."

By the time Avery dropped her off at the art store, the sun shone high in a bright blue sky and the temperature had risen above freezing. "If I don't see you again, it was nice meeting you," Lillian said as she opened the car door. "Thank you for a nice morning."

"My pleasure. I was a stranger in town not long ago and remember how alone I felt until I met a few people. If you decide to stick around a little longer, give me or Nan a call."

"I'll see how it goes. Tell the sheriff hi for me."

Avery waved and pulled away as Lillian entered the store, the sharp, nose tickling scent of paints turning her fingers itchy to get back to work. With everything that had happened in the past week, it was doubtful she would still attend the Naples Art Show next week, and that was a good thing. Given her frame of mind, she wouldn't have made a favorable impression on anyone even if the work she planned to enter was some of her best.

She spent two hours in the store and made the owner's day with her purchases. After arranging to have them delivered to the motel, she set out on foot, figuring she could call Bob if she got too cold or tired before reaching the motel. The walk was necessary to clear her head as she couldn't help the images planted in her mind from listening to Avery and Nan describe their husbands and relationships with them. After what Brad had subjected her to with his blackmailed control, she couldn't imagine ever becoming a willing partner in such a relationship. It didn't matter that her body grew warm and tingly when she thought of turning herself over to Mitchell's dominant care. If she went off like a firecracker from having his hands on and in her, what would it be like to give herself over to his fully controlled possession?

Lillian shuddered as she imagined the possible heights he could drive her to. Lifting her face to the sun, she let the rays add additional warmth to her overheated body. There was no way of knowing if her strong, uncharacteristic reaction that night had been due to stress and/or grief, or a buildup of needy lust. She never denied Mitchell was an attractive, sexy man even if his bossy attitude turned her off. What turned her on had been those light slaps that left her aching for more and his talented fingers invading her body with ruthless determination and possession, wringing multiple orgasms from her before he was through.

After reaching the motel and letting Bob know she didn't need the ride, Lillian warmed up in the shower and spent the rest of the afternoon painting. She was so immersed in her art, she jumped when her phone buzzed and Nan asked if she wanted to go to dinner.

"Is it that late already?" Glancing at the time, she saw it was almost six.

"Yes, and I'm starving. Dan will be at least another hour and Gertie's special is fried shrimp tonight. I can be there in ten minutes to get you."

"I'll be ready. Thanks, Nan."

"Don't just stand there expectin' me to escort you to a seat. Grab a stool."

Nan smiled at the scowling older woman bustling behind the

long counter inside Dale's Diner. "Gertie, be nice. Lillian is stranded here until Mort gets her car fixed."

Lillian eyed the crotchety woman with a bemused expression as she took a seat next to Nan. The corner diner resembling something out of the fifties with its black and white checkered floor and juke boxes in every booth was almost full, and if the food was half as good as it smelled, she understood why.

Slapping a menu down in front of her, Gertie gave her bruised face a critical once over before nodding, as if coming to some kind of conclusion about her. "I see our doc took good care of you. Next time, don't be out on those back roads with weather coming in. There's still shrimp left, if you want the special."

"I take it Gertie's sparkling personality is why this place is so popular," Lillian drawled with humorous sarcasm as Gertie turned to grab two filled plates off the shelf separating the kitchen from the counter.

"Don't let her fool you. She blusters a lot but has a heart as big as Montana. She gave Avery a job when she came to town alone and almost broke and never asked questions when Avery said she needed to be paid in cash. Instead, she offered to let her stay in the upstairs apartment as part of her salary."

"I sense a story there." Lillian scanned the menu, leaving it up to Nan whether to say more about how Avery had come to Willow Springs.

"Yes, but it's hers to tell. It ended well for her, though, and she snagged our hot sheriff to boot."

A shudder rippled through her as she recalled Sheriff Monroe's icy glare when he saw her face. "He's a little scary, and I don't scare easily."

Nan chuckled. "Like our Gertie, Grayson's glare and sharp mouth is mostly bluster. I wouldn't attempt to rub him the wrong way at the club, but I'd trust him with my life, and to have my back, just as I would any of my friends, including Doctor Hoffstetter. C'mon, Lillian," she coaxed with an elbow nudge. "Spill about you and Mitchell. No red-blooded woman could stay closed up with him for long and not beg to get naked with him."

"You're married," Lillian reminded her with an arched brow.

"But I'm not dead. I can look and fantasize."

Gertie returned and they ordered the special, giving Lillian a minute to gather her thoughts. A change of subject was definitely in order. "Sorry, but there's nothing to tell, like I said earlier. And if he's a member of that club, I now know why we didn't hit it off. No offense, but that's not my thing." Waving a hand around her face, she said bluntly, "One man beating on me was enough for a lifetime." Which didn't explain why she'd responded so strongly to those teasing butt taps.

"Yeah, and I'm sorry for you. I have experience with an abuser myself, and could tell you there's a world of difference, like comparing apples to oranges, but it's something that can't be explained. You either see it, experience it and know, or you don't." Nan paused as Gertie set their plates in front of them.

"There you go. Eat up, you're both too skinny."

"You don't have to tell me twice. Thanks, Gertie." Nan bit into a large, crusted shrimp and then changed the subject, much to Lillian's relief. "Where are you headed once you get your car back?"

Anywhere. Nowhere. "I haven't decided yet. Once I was free of that jerk, I just took off."

Nan nodded. "I get that. Sometimes running without looking back or forward is easier than staying still and learning to adjust."

Lillian dropped a shrimp tail on the plate, eyeing her askance. "Is that what you did, learned to adjust?"

"Nope, just the opposite. I stayed still and *didn't* cope, not as well as I'd thought, even after counseling. Thankfully, my friends, Dan being the most important, showed me the error of my thinking and then offered me unconditional support. You know, Lillian, if you don't have anywhere you have to be, you could do worse than hanging around here for a while."

She scooped up a forkful of mashed potatoes then paused to reply, "And how long would that take to get around?"

"Hey, cut us some slack," Nan protested with a wide grin. "It's winter and we get bored."

"Glad my mishap could entertain everyone. Trust me, Mitchell wasn't entertained." And why that caused her chest to tighten, she hadn't a clue.

"Now that I believe. Our good doctor likes to keep his distance."

"Except at your club?"

Nan shrugged. "Well, yeah. There, he gives his play partner his full attention and no one has walked away from a scene unhappy. He's still grieving for his wife."

Liana's laughing face popped into Lillian's head and a pang gripped her stomach. Grief she could commiserate with and now understood Mitchell's compassionate patience with her presence better. It seemed they shared one thing in common after all. "Yeah," she sighed, "that must be rough."

Mitchell returned to his Craftsman house on an acre of land just inside Willow Springs city limits Saturday morning, a day earlier than he'd planned, and he wasn't happy about it. Grabbing his duffel out of the back of his Tahoe, he flicked the garage door opener before walking out and crossing the drive to enter the house through the side door. After cranking up the heat, he poured himself a stiff whiskey and padded over to an eight-by-ten-inch picture of Abbie perched on the fireplace mantle. The quiet retreat he'd planned around their anniversary had been interrupted and then, because he was spending more time thinking about a pair of haunted purple eyes instead of his wife's loving blue gaze, frustration prompted him to cut it short. And that did not sit well with him.

He'd met Abbie at a Valentine's party at a Denver club,

married her on February fourteenth a year later and she died on February fifteenth seven years after that. Eight years was not enough; at the time, he'd thought a lifetime wouldn't be enough. Looking at her shy expression, cloud of blonde hair and bright blue eyes, she was nothing like Lillian, and yet, he found himself comparing the two women way too much after saying goodbye to Lillian.

The flashes of pain-driven determination he'd caught crossing her bruised face more than once got to him in a way he couldn't define, at least, not yet. Whatever the extent of that bastard's abuse, she didn't cower from it, and he didn't care for the pinch of guilt pricking his conscience whenever he questioned whether he should have pressed her for answers. *None of my business.* That's what he'd been telling himself since bringing her into his cabin. He didn't want to get involved with her or her problems, so why had he wrestled with sleep the past few nights, and why couldn't he shove aside the regret and shame he'd caught in her dark eyes before she would don a polite mask of indifference?

"You know, baby," he murmured to Abbie's picture as he traced a finger over her face, "I think you would have liked Lillian's grit in the face of her trauma. You were always more compassionate than me."

Mitchell remembered Lillian's anger when he'd called her baby, and the defiance etched on her pale face as she lay in the snow under him and refuted being raped. He wasn't a shrink, but there was no arguing the woman was bottled up tight in denial. But again, not his problem. She was likely gone by now, hundreds of miles away and possibly giving him the finger in the rearview mirror. Why that image tugged at the corners of his mouth, he couldn't imagine.

Tossing back his whiskey, he strode to the antique roll top desk in the corner and flipped through a week's worth of mail. Seeing nothing pressing, he considered giving his mother a call and then opted to put it off until the next day. He and his sister couldn't have asked for better parents growing up, and now that his dad was gone and he'd made the move to Montana, he made sure he kept in touch with both of them.

Mitchell grabbed his bag of dirty clothes and carried it into the laundry room off the kitchen, which was in the middle of a renovation. He'd purchased the dated house for a good price and spent his down time remodeling, which was why it was taking so long. He'd left Denver, and his prestigious position as the head of a trauma center, for a slower, calmer pace of life, hoping the drastic change would help him move on from losing Abbie. Now, over eight months later, the jury was still out on whether that was the right decision.

After starting a load of wash, Mitchell debated whether to go out for something to eat or settle for a frozen dinner and opted for the diner, which was as good as a home-cooked meal. Afterward, maybe he would drive out to The Barn and socialize. He enjoyed his new friends and their private club even more than the people and venue he'd left behind. Here, there were no pitying looks or well-meaning condolences that kept his grief at the forefront. The changes he'd made in his life hadn't been easy, but overall, the small town of Willow Springs and the people who welcomed him into their close-knit group were proving a good fit for him.

Neither snow nor frigid temperatures kept people home much in Montana, as demonstrated when Mitchell parked in front of Dale's Diner an hour later and he could see the Saturday night crowd through the window. Hungry for Gertie's chicken fried steak smothered in cream gravy, he entered the diner looking for an empty seat or someone he could join at their table. Instead, his eyes zeroed in on the woman perched at the counter, her cascade of dark auburn hair familiar enough to give him a jolt.

Why the hell was Lillian Gillespie still in town?

"Grab that last stool at the counter, Doc, and I'll be right with you," Barbara, the waitress tossed out as she breezed by him carrying a laden tray. "We're swamped tonight."

"Thanks, and no hurry, Barbara." Seeing no way out of it, not if he wanted to eat tonight, Mitchell slid onto the seat next to Lillian, removed his hat and tunneled his fingers through his hair. Her small gasp indicated she was as surprised to see him as he was at finding her here. "Didn't Mort get your car fixed?" Those striking eyes narrowed, and her soft lips tightened in annoyance. Yeah, that sounded rude, but he'd been unprepared for his gut-wrenching reaction at seeing her again.

"Yes, he did. I wasn't aware that meant I had to leave right away," she stated in a frigid tone.

He sighed, reaching up to squeeze her shoulder. "Sorry, I didn't mean that the way it sounded. I wasn't expecting to see you here, is all."

She shrugged under his hand and averted her eyes. "I didn't plan on sticking around, but I met a few people who convinced me this was a nice place to hang for a while." She faced him again, a rueful smile tugging at her lips. "Don't worry, Doctor Hoffstetter, I promise not to intrude on your space."

Gertie snatched a steaming plate off the ledge and set it down in front of Lillian in time to hear her remark. Scowling, she pointed a finger at Mitchell. "Are you being rude to one of my customers?"

"No, ma'am, I leave that up to you," he drawled. "I'd like the chicken fried steak with the works, please."

"*Hmmph*, as if I didn't already know that." Turning her back on them, she called out, "Get me another special, Ed!"

A wide smile lightened Lillian's face and Mitchell was taken aback by how it transformed her from cute to eye-catching attractive. The smattering of freckles decorating her pert nose below her large, expressive eyes added to the overall appeal of her looks, but the fading, yellow-tinged bruises reminded him of her troubles.

"She's one of the reasons I like coming in here. I get a kick out of her. She has a knack for making you feel welcome while grumbling." Looking at her plate filled with meatloaf, baked potato and green beans, Lillian added, "And she insists on giving me enough food for three meals."

Thinking to make up for his earlier insensitivity, he waited until she swallowed a bite of meatloaf before running a finger over her marred cheek. "Want me to beat him up for you?"

She leaned into his hand without realizing it and Mitchell's cock stirred with an unwelcome quick jolt of lust. "Not necessary but thanks."

Controlling himself, he trailed his finger down to the small cut in the corner of her mouth. "The person who did this, was he a friend then lover before revealing his true nature? That's often how abusive relationships begin."

She paled at that question and then reddened as she moved her head enough to lose his touch. "He's an asshole who enjoys wielding power over people to get what he wants."

Shame colored her tone and the urge to pound on something tightened his abdomen in a response he understood and accepted. "And he wanted you. Did your relationship with him have anything to do with your sister's death?" The spasm of grief that turned Lillian's eyes watery cut Mitchell to the quick. He knew how a casual inquiry could stir up the misery of loss. Maybe he wasn't the one to get her to open up and face her demons.

The doctor couldn't have asked a better question to defuse Lillian's heated response to seeing him again. Every cell in her body had gone on high alert when he'd taken a seat next to her, his large body so close all she could think about was when he'd set aside his irritation long enough to help her cope with her sorrow. She blinked back the tears before they fell and strove to get herself under control. His question hit too near to the truth for comfort. Brad might not have been directly responsible for Liana's death, but she would always blame him for taking advantage of her sister's medical condition to get what he wanted from

Lillian. She'd caved to his blackmail because he'd left her no choice, but that didn't lessen the shame of putting up with his abuse for those four weeks instead of telling him to go to Hell.

"I don't want to discuss him, or Liana."

Mitchell was diverted from answering when Ed, one of the cooks, called out, "Order up!" Gertie plucked the plate off the shelf and set it in front of him without a word before shuffling down the counter to another customer.

Cutting into his meat, he nodded, saying, "Good enough, but you should talk to someone." She opened her mouth to retort it was none of his business but he cut her off with a piercing look. "Eat before it gets cold."

"I see you're as bossy as you were at the cabin." Nonetheless, she was hungry and turned her attention back to her food.

"It comes with being responsible for people's health."

Thanks to Nan telling her about their private club, Lillian knew that wasn't the whole of it. That bossy dominance extended past his patients' wellbeing. Wasn't it bad enough her imagination had run rampant the past few days with picturing this man at a kink club dishing out erotic torment on trussed up women? Must she suffer his close presence and those narrow-eyed, probing looks that stirred her in odd, new ways again? She supposed if she was going to stick around Willow Springs for another few weeks she should get used to running into the well-liked doctor. With the town population just over seven thousand, there would be no avoiding him unless she planned to stay holed up in the motel room. After visiting all the local shops, meeting the friendly, welcoming townsfolk and sharing afternoon tea with Nan the last four days, the thought of keeping to herself held no appeal.

"That might be part of it, Doc, but not all. I'm not your patient now," she said before diving into the creamy mound of potatoes. If she kept eating in the diner every night, she was going to have to buy a whole new wardrobe soon.

"Yes, you are. In fact, since you intend to stay longer, why don't you come to the clinic on Monday? I'd like to confirm my diagnosis by getting x-rays of your ribs. Are you still at the motel?"

"Yes, but I suppose it would be cheaper to find a short-term rental until I make some decisions. And I'm fine," she insisted. "I don't need x-rays."

What I don't need is his hands on me again. So far, she couldn't forget that one hour and the multiple orgasms he wrung from her, or the surprising stimulation of those butt slaps and nipple pinches. That wasn't like her. There'd never been a man she couldn't walk away from, or a sexual encounter she couldn't easily forget once it was over. That *he* was the first man to leave a lasting impression made her uneasy since he was so far removed from the type she was usually drawn to.

"I'll make you a deal." *Don't do it.* Mitchell's inner warning voice had him pausing, but only for a second. Lillian still winced when she moved, and that worried him, but admitted that was no reason to offer her the apartment above his garage while she was in town. So why was he opening his mouth to do just that? "I have a small studio apartment above my garage. You're free to use it in exchange for coming by next week and getting those x-rays. What do you say?"

He held his breath as she looked at him with suspicion. "You couldn't wait to get me out of your cabin."

"That was my private retreat during some much-needed alone time. The garage is separate from the house. You won't have to see me except for one visit to the clinic." He shrugged with a sigh, as much in wonder at himself for the offer as to convey it was no big deal to ease her mind. "It'll save you some money and maybe make it easier to take your time deciding where you want to go from here. But, I'll hold you to coming by for a checkup."

Lillian toyed with her green beans, took a drink of water and then finally nodded her head. "Okay, it's a deal."

Reaching into his back pocket, he pulled out a note pad and

jotted down his address and the easy directions to his place from the motel. He handed the paper and a key to her. "I'll be gone until early afternoon tomorrow, so if you come on over after one, I'll help you upstairs with your things."

"This is nice of you. Thank you."

He could tell she was as unsure about accepting the offer as he was about making it. Maybe that was why he found it easier to justify his uncharacteristic gesture. Or maybe it was time he quit letting his grief keep him from putting himself out for others.

"You can thank me by getting those x-rays." Mitchell was sure he could put Lillian and the need she didn't know was reflected on her face every time her sister or the ass that abused her was mentioned out of his mind once he confirmed her physical well-being.

Chapter 6

Nan's eyes widened in surprise as she handed Lillian the steaming teacup and then settled on the chair across the table from her. "Are you honestly going to sit there and continue to insist there's nothing between you and Mitchell?"

"I think she is," Avery answered when Lillian shook her head. "Deny it all you want, Lillian, but for a man who doesn't get involved on a personal level with anyone, an offer to stay in his apartment from our sexy doctor is huge."

"It's only for a short time, and the apartment is above his detached garage. I haven't seen him all week, so it's not like we're bumping into each other all the time." Lillian sipped the cinnamon flavored black tea, enjoying the flavor more than her new friend's inquisitiveness. She winced as she realized she hadn't kept her side of their bargain yet by making an appointment with Mitchell for a checkup.

Last Sunday, she had moved into the apartment without waiting for his help. Not only did it go against her independent nature to idly sit back at his insistence when there was no need, but every time she was around the man, her libido took over her common sense and threw her emotions and her body into turmoil. Didn't she have enough on her mind with coming to terms with the loss of her twin and the degradation of sharing Brad's bed after his abuse to keep Liana safe from his threats? It still baffled her how she could have responded without hesitation to Mitchell's touch so soon after walking away from that jerk. Still, she would have to find time to stop in at the clinic and keep her promise to get those x-rays.

"Just the invitation to stay on his property is enough to tweak our curiosity. He's friendly and all, but so far he's kept himself at arm's length from the members at the club he's scened with, and hasn't accepted any invitations to socialize outside of the club," Nan said.

Uncomfortable with the way her stomach knotted at the mention of Mitchell with those other women, Lillian shifted on the seat and toyed with the dainty teacup handle as she replied, "Sorry to burst your bubble yet again, but we're just friendly acquaintances."

Avery and Nan exchanged a look and Avery shrugged, saying, "That's too bad. We were hoping you might be the one to help him get over losing his wife."

Lillian sat back, releasing her breath on a sigh. That was a turn in the conversation she could relate to and felt the need to defend Mitchell. "Having just lost my twin sister and only relative, I can tell you it's not easy to move on. I can't imagine losing a spouse, but you two should understand how he might feel."

Both girls paled slightly. "You're right, Lillian. Dan and I were friends and occasional lovers for five years, but now that we're *in* love, being without him is unimaginable," Nan admitted.

"Yeah, what Nan said. Other than the social worker who would take me in whenever my mom went back to drinking and couldn't take care of me, I was alone in the world until I came here and met Grayson and then everyone else. I'm sorry for your loss, Lillian. Losing a twin must be awful." Avery reached over and squeezed her arm and Lillian blinked back the tears that could still form and blur her vision with little provocation. "Okay, let's talk about something else. If you're not busy a week from tomorrow night, our friend, Sydney said to invite you for chili at their ranch. It's just us and Tamara and Connor."

The invitation spread a pleasant glow through Lillian, who was touched at being included. It would be nice not to spend an evening alone, missing Liana so much she ached and coping with the loss of the only close, special relationship she'd ever had. She hurried to accept before the lifestyle they shared in common and she knew little about and had no interest in gave her pause.

"Thank you, if you're sure your friend doesn't mind. I could pick up a bottle of wine. Oh, sorry, Avery. I assume you're not drinking for the next few months," she said, remembering her pregnancy.

Nan spoke up before Avery could answer. "She's not, and neither are Sydney and Tamara, but I am and I say, yes please."

Avery gave her a mock glare. "You just wait. We have plans to get even." Turning to Lillian, she said, "She's rubbed it in at every girl's night since Sydney and Tamara got pregnant eight months ago."

Nan didn't look worried as she bit into a sugar cookie. "I'm betting Kelsey beats me to it, after all, sharing a bed with two men offers twice the opportunities to plant that seed."

The bell above the teashop door chimed as two women entered and took a seat. Nan rose to wait on the newcomers, a twinkle in her eyes as she smiled at Lillian. "If you get a chance to meet both her guys and don't envy Kelsey, there's something seriously wrong with you. You can ride out to the Dunbar's with me when I close up here and stay overnight at our place afterward, if you want. Just let me know next week."

She wasn't a prude, but the images popping into Lillian's head flushed her face with heat as Nan walked away and she turned toward Avery. "*Two?*"

"Oh, yeah." Avery fanned herself with an impish grin.

Lillian returned her smile and then asked, "What else can I bring that you and your friends can have?"

"Nothing, we're good." Avery rose with her. "Sydney was a chef at a fancy restaurant before moving here, and now she cooks for all the hands on the Dunbar ranch. She'd be offended if you brought something, even a bottle of wine, and trust me, anything she makes is great."

"Then I look forward to it, and to meeting your friends. Thank you for inviting me." She waved to Nan before walking out with Avery.

"I have to put in a few hours at the IT office in Billings this afternoon. What are your plans?" Avery asked, fishing her keys out of her purse.

"Painting. I'm behind and there are a few shows I want to attend this spring and summer."

Avery's eyes brightened with interest. "Don't leave town before I get a chance to see your work."

The afternoon sun warmed her face as Lillian opened her car door, lifting her hand in agreement. "Come by any time."

With a wave, Avery pulled out and Lillian drove in the opposite direction toward Mitchell's street, unsettled by the pang she experienced when Avery mentioned her leaving. She'd hung around Willow Springs for two weeks and the welcome she received from everyone she'd met had put a crack in the ice surrounding her heart that left her so cold following Liana's death. The way Nan and Avery had pulled her into a quick friendship even though she was just passing through had prompted her to linger in the small pleasant town, and then she'd seen Mitchell again.

As she parked in front of his garage and her thoughts switched to her temporary landlord, she wondered how much he had played into her staying so long. Other than last Sunday evening when he'd come up to ask if there was anything she needed, she'd only seen him from the upstairs window as he left for work each morning. His face had been stamped with disapproval when he'd chided her for not waiting for his help to haul her things up the stairs, but then he'd let her be, just as she had him. That hadn't kept her dreams from continuing to relive that one hour in his cabin when his hard hands had delivered the most powerful orgasms of her experience.

"I might have to move on just to forget that night, and that damn man," she muttered, entering the cozy apartment and shucking her coat. A Murphy bed was folded up against the wall and a small sofa faced a television mounted on the opposite wall. The compact kitchenette with apartment-size appliances took up the third wall space with the bathroom and a closet located off a short hallway. The one large window offered a wide view of the open fields behind the street and a glimpse of the side driveway. The piles of snow from the blizzard two weeks ago were already melted down to small mounds here and there with peeks of dried grass showing. White swirls of snow decorated the far-off mountain peaks and she could only imagine the stunning view come summer.

Turning away from the vista and the thought of so far in the future, Lillian settled behind her easel set up in front of the window and got back to work. If anything could keep her from fantasizing about another scene with the country doctor, losing herself in her art could.

That evening, Lillian started a new painting off a picture she'd taken of Mitchell's cabin, and was still immersed in putting that scene on canvas late the next day, Friday afternoon. Something about the rustic abode with its backdrop of ice crystal-draped trees and plume of smoke traveling up into the gray sky appealed to her. Before getting stranded there with him, the closest she'd gotten to roughing it was when she and Liana spent a week at a Colorado ski resort, complete with their own private hot tub and an indoor pool. She was quite proud of herself for handling the tight, drafty quarters, limited hot water and basic meals so well, not to mention her autocratic but considerate rescuer. Those off the charts orgasms likely lessened the memory of how uncomfortable those few days were.

The heavy clomp of feet tromping up the side staircase

reached her ears as she noticed the time. It ceased surprising her how fast the hours flew by unnoticed when she couldn't pull herself away from her work.

Mitchell's irritated voice followed a sharp rap on the door. "Lillian, I need to talk to you."

Even annoyed his deep baritone could deliver that warm rush she had never experienced with another man, and *that* irked *her*. Striding to the door, she flung it open with a glare. A shiver went through her, but whether from the cold air or the swirling emotion turning his hazel eyes more brown than green, she wasn't sure. Reminding herself this was his place and she was staying here for free, Lillian lightened her frown and stepped back to let him in.

"What's up? Did I disobey some unspoken rule of tenancy?"

Mitchell brushed by her, his sheepskin coat flapping open to reveal he was still dressed in slacks and a button up shirt, the attire she'd seen him wearing every morning as he left for the clinic. The fact she couldn't help glancing out the window at exactly 7:30 a.m. every day this past week was another deviation from her character that puzzled her.

He turned to face her as she closed the door, fisting his hands on his hips. "No, you reneged on our bargain."

Puzzled, Lillian searched her memory and then recalled the appointment she was supposed to make at his clinic, realizing he was right. *Oops*. She shrugged and offered him a self-deprecating smile. "Not on purpose. I meant to, but I started a new painting and completely forgot." Instead of forgiving her, Mitchell narrowed his eyes, his reply amusing her even as it sent a small thrill trickling through her veins.

"Someone should have taken you in hand years ago."

With her hair pulled up in a scraggly ponytail, a smudge of white paint on her face, a pinched frown between her eyes and her cute bare feet showing below her long skirt, Mitchell's first glimpse of Lillian all week struck him like a sucker punch to the stomach. The paint-spattered, loose flannel shirt she wore untucked from the denim skirt was a sloppy deviation from the winter wool slacks and dressy sweaters he'd seen her in before. And yet, his quicksilver response was the same.

All week he'd checked his schedule and watched the clinic's doors for her to keep the appointment she'd promised him. More than concern for a patient had prodded him into obsessing over her continued absence, and he'd fought against confronting her until closing today. Giving up the battle, he figured she would argue she didn't need the x-rays or checkup, thus giving him a good reason to put her out of his mind once and for all.

Instead, she shook him with that small taunting smile and admitted her fault. Why couldn't she act in a predictable manner and make dealing with her easier? Like at the cabin, one minute she would berate him for being bossy and the next, start a playful snowball fight without warning. He sure as hell wasn't prepared for the gleam that entered her eyes and tilt of her head as she smirked with a comeback that rattled his control.

"Gee, Doc, do you want to spank me?"

Mitchell could tell she didn't take that comment seriously, but he did. His palm still tingled whenever he recalled the warmth of her soft buttocks after he'd delivered those light smacks at the cabin and it itched now for a repeat. He needed to turn the tables on her fast and delegate her to the status of every other woman he'd scened with since losing his beloved Abbie. That of a submissive acquaintance.

Taking a step forward, he cupped her chin and held her head up, keeping her eyes on him as he replied, "In the worst way, pet. I enjoyed playing with your ass before and wouldn't mind another chance, especially if it leads to you keeping your end of our bargain and getting those x-rays."

Surprise and a flare of heat entered her direct gaze, but he could see her fighting against remembering the arousal his touch had produced. She jerked against his grip and he released her. The rapid fluttering of her pulse in her neck was enough to prove how much he'd affected her.

Her slim brows dipped into another frown. "It was an honest memory lapse, not a deliberate attempt to go back on my word. I'm not one of those women who wants to kneel at your feet and let you dictate to me."

Lillian took a step back and Mitchell moved forward, refusing to let her off the hook yet. "Afraid you won't measure up? You needn't be. I don't compare." Her shoulders went rigid and back, a telling sign she didn't back down from a challenge. Good to know.

The taunting smile returned. "I'm not afraid of any man. Just ask my ex."

"Don't mention that ass to me," he warned in a hard tone. The bruises might appear almost gone, but he would always remember his first look at the trauma inflicted upon her delicate features. She took another step in retreat, and he followed. "If that's the case, then I can only surmise you're afraid you'll like it. You didn't complain or stop me last time." Mitchell questioned his sanity in needling her but couldn't seem to stop himself.

Bumping up against the couch, Lillian waved a hand with a shake of her head. "That was foreplay. Is that what you're suggesting? Because I might go for that."

Mitchell chuckled, enjoying the back and forth with her. It was something he hadn't done with a woman since his preference for dominant control took over his sexual encounters about fifteen years ago. He could tell she couldn't decide whether to be peeved or amused by the suggestion. His chest tightened as he once again found he needed to put her in the same category as the others, even if she wasn't a submissive.

In a move that caught her unaware, he snatched her hand, sank down onto the couch and yanked her over his knees, taking a chance this would do the trick for both of them. "I'm thinking more along the lines of a disciplinary lesson that will help you remember to keep your promise the next time. Lie still."

She stuttered on a laugh, whipping her head around to look up at him with bright eyes. "This is ridiculous. A grown woman lying over a man's lap like a recalcitrant child."

"I figured you would berate me for being bossy again." Placing a hand on her butt, he kneaded the soft flesh through her calf-length skirt and watched her eyes darken with arousal as she stiffened. "You're definitely not a child." He never claimed to play fair.

Lillian struggled with dual responses to Mitchell's highhandedness and coaxing touch. It was difficult to discern which was strongest, the hot gush pooling between her legs from that intent gaze and fondling hand, or the need to prove she didn't go for the dominant, bossy type as she'd claimed. He settled the matter in the next second, while their eyes were still locked and he slid down her thigh to inch up her skirt. The cool air wafting over her exposed legs didn't temper the heat spreading from her face to her toes.

"I'm not sure this is a good idea." Before, he'd caught her in a vulnerable state of grieving and she'd assumed that accounted for giving in to his touch so easily. Yet now, the brush of that calloused palm up her bare thigh was enough to stir her arousal to the same feverish pitch, negating that excuse.

"I suggest you decide quickly." He inched further up her leg and rested his hand at the crease where thigh met the under curve of her buttock, one finger swiping the sensitive skin just under her panties. "You're not afraid, right?"

Lillian narrowed her eyes at the provocation. Growing up, it had always been she who loved issuing challenges, especially to her more timid sister. There was a heady rush, she was learning, to taking on a dare just to prove a point.

"Like I said, Doc, I don't fear any man. Do your worst." Flipping her head back down, she wiggled her hips and held her breath.

"You couldn't handle my worst, pet," Mitchell drawled as he lifted his hand and smacked her cheek. The slight sting came and went, leaving behind a warm pulse that curbed her tongue. "But let's see how you take a little more than the taps I gave you before."

I'll show him. I can... "Ow!" Lillian reached around and rubbed her butt where he delivered a spank hard enough to burn. Shoving aside her hand, he caressed the pain away, that soft rub going a long way in defusing her annoyance and dampening her sheath. *That's just not right*, she bemoaned as her pussy fluttered in a cream-drenched response.

"My memory hasn't failed me," he said as he spanked her again. "Your ass has an enticing bounce and your muscle tone," he squeezed one globe, "is firm but still soft. I like that."

Lillian gripped his calf as he lowered her panties and bared her buttocks. "Gee, I'm so glad you approve of my butt." She had intended sarcasm but her voice wobbled with the lust slowly roiling through her veins when he cupped her naked flesh.

"I would say I'm an ass man but there's nothing about a woman's body I don't like." He took a moment to trail his hand down one leg and back up the other, his light touch raising goosebumps in its wake and her awareness of her vulnerable display by the time he returned to her cheeks. "Take a breath."

She bristled at the command and then swore as his hard hand connected with her bare skin with enough force to demonstrate the difference between teasing slaps and a real spanking. Heat blossomed across her buttock, the sting once again sliding away as fast as his hand had landed. If the pain lingered longer, went deeper, she was sure she could have fought off responding to it. It went against everything inside her, everything she'd ever believed about herself and her desire to feel her pussy swell and spasm with the next smack. Heat flooded her sheath along with another gush of cream as the next slap echoed along with her gasp. She wiggled her hips again, this time seeking relief from the increasing waves of throbbing, hot pulses moving up and down her vagina in tune with those rippling across her buttocks.

Mitchell gave her one more smack and then casually roamed over the flesh he had just reddened. "You tempt me to push your limits, Lillian, and that's not a good idea."

No, it's not. She hadn't been prepared to respond so strongly this time, and that was before he shifted his caressing hand down between her legs and trailed a finger over her slit. This wasn't like her, to lie docilely over a man's lap and let him do whatever he wanted, but, damn, she craved that finger moving inside her drenched, aching pussy.

Turning her face up again, she shook her hair out of her eyes. "Told you I wasn't afraid. Now, don't I get a reward?" She pressed her pelvis down, against the finger he refused to move again.

Shaking his head, a rueful smile tugged at his lips. "You are *so* not what I expected." With his eyes pinned on hers, he thrust inside her.

"Oh, God." Hiding her face again, Lillian lifted into Mitchell's next deep stroke, the press of his palm and thumb against her sore cheek igniting the warmth and emphasizing the continuing throbbing. Lillian shivered as he circled her clit and then groaned with his sharp tug on that tender nub. Small contractions convulsed her swollen inner muscles and increased with each, tormenting yank of her clit.

"Now, pet. Come on my finger."

The order grated but there was no ignoring the erotic demand. A mortifying whimper slipped past her tightened lips as she arched into his now pummeling fingers, squeezing them with her inner muscles as a climax burst in a fanfare of bright sparks and sweat-inducing pleasure. Her head whirled and buzzed as her entire body went up in a blaze of ecstasy. By the time she floated down from the incredible high and realized she was lying over his knees in a quivering, sated heap, her chest heaving as

Mitchell calmed her with slow, almost casual strokes inside her, a different kind of mortification took over.

Lillian stiffened, rolled off his lap and got to her feet. Keeping her face averted, she pulled up her panties, grousing, "I told you not to call me pet." Dropping her skirt, she looked at him as he rose and she noticed he still wore his coat. For some reason, that added to the humiliation of succumbing to him as easily as she imagined the women at his club did.

"I keep forgetting. I'll try to do better."

He looked serious, as if he meant it, but she doubted it. "See that you do. I have to get back to work."

Without arguing, Mitchell strode to the door, tossing over his shoulder, "Monday morning, 9:00 at the clinic."

After he shut the door behind him, Lillian mimicked in a mock voice, "Monday morning, 9:00 at the clinic. That man is way too domineering for my tastes." But as she settled on the seat behind her easel and moaned from the pressure on her still sensitive butt, she couldn't prevent a grin of satisfaction. "Bossy, yes, but boy, can he deliver."

"How was your getaway week?"

Mitchell glanced at his friend, Kurt Wilcox, as the rancher took the bar stool next to him. Soft cries following the snap of leather against bare skin resonated down from the loft above them where a few couples were enjoying the BDSM equipment of their private club, The Barn. Behind the bar, others were gyrating to the beat of the music on the dance floor. The smile tugging at the corners of Kurt's mouth hinted he had heard about his guest and distracted him from watching Master Brett grip his wife's bare ass under her short skirt as they ground their pelvises together while dancing.

"Wipe that smirk off your face, Wilcox. It went just fine."

"Yeah, sounds like it. Nothing like a bruised, stranded young woman to liven up your week off work." Kurt turned serious with a frown. "She wasn't hurt too bad?"

"Bad enough since her injuries were caused by her ex. At least she walked away and wasn't making excuses for him. That was a refreshing change from the cases that came into the hospital back home." And was just one of Lillian's admirable traits that kept him thinking about her. "Where's Leslie? I'm surprised you let her out of your sight. Aren't you still driving her into school every day?"

"After I kept her bound on the fucking swing for an hour, I thought she could use a long soak in the hot tub with Kelsey. And yes, I'm taking her into work despite her arguments every morning. It's going to take me longer to get over the scare of almost losing her than it has her." Kurt shifted his black gaze out the back glass sliding door where they could both make out the girls' heads and bobbing breasts above the rim of the bubbling spa.

Mitchell reached out and squeezed Kurt's shoulder. Fear of losing that one person who completes you is something he could sympathize with. The heart-shattering pain of those first months following Abbie's death might have eased into a dull ache after two years, but he would never stop missing her, or what they had together. Lillian's grief-stricken face as she'd stood in the yellow/orange glow of the blazing fire popped into his head, followed by her bright eyes lit with humor as she wiggled on his lap. His abdomen cramped, as if thinking about Lillian betrayed his wife's memory.

Gritting his teeth, he replied, "Yeah, I get that," before changing the subject. "I was proud of your dad for working so hard while you and Leslie spent most of her semester break with her sister in Canada. I never expected him to recover to such a degree following his stroke. His determination, when he finally got around to applying himself, really paid off."

"I'm proud of him too, but let's get back to discussing this redhead I've heard about. Did you really offer her your garage apartment?"

Mitchell couldn't fault Kurt for the disbelief coloring his tone. The simple gesture of letting Lillian use the room above the garage was the first time he'd reached out to anyone in the last eight months of living in Willow Springs. He'd met Kurt when he'd become Leland Wilcox's doctor following the older man's stroke. Through him, he'd become acquainted with the owners of The Barn and its members. He enjoyed the new friendships and the weekend nights he spent with willing partners who desired dominant sexual control, but had refrained from expanding on any relationship outside the renovated barn's walls beyond a casual dinner at the diner once in a while.

He'd found it harder to move on by starting over in a new place, with a new, less stressful job than he'd imagined. And then he'd met Lillian, who was the complete opposite of what he always looked for in a suitable sexual partner.

"Yes," he finally answered, twirling the amber liquor in his glass. "That space has sat empty since I bought the place. It didn't make sense to let her pay for a much smaller motel room for weeks when she could stay there. Don't make a big deal out of it," he warned his friend. "It doesn't mean anything. It's not like I invited her to move in with me."

"And yet you haven't been here the last two weekends and there you sit, disappointing the subs you've turned away the last two hours," Kurt drawled as Grayson, who was bartending, strolled up from behind the mahogany bar top.

Plunking down a cold brew in front of Kurt, the sheriff pinned Mitchell with his gray/green gaze. "We hear enough complaints from them about the dwindling number of uncommitted Doms to see to their needs without you turning them away."

Last Saturday, after seeing Lillian again, he'd returned home for a quiet night contemplating his stupidity in inviting her to stay on his property after he'd sworn he was glad when Grayson had taken her off his hands. The woman had played havoc with his emotions and his intentions since he'd first clapped eyes on her bruised, defiant face. He didn't have a reason for turning away the subs that had approached him in the last two hours other than he refused to do a scene with one of them when his mind was on someone else.

"There are still several single members to take care of their needs." Sipping his whiskey, a strident yelp drew his gaze to the occupied spanking bench on the other side of the bar and the bright red ass trying to shift away from the descending paddle. He recalled Lillian's cushiony cheeks turning pink under his hand, the way she went from struggling to staying put to lifting for the next swat, and his cock stirred for the first time that night.

He cut his eyes back to his friends. "Besides, the night isn't over, now is it?"

Kurt held up a placating hand. "Okay, don't get pissed. On a different note, will you be at Caden's Friday night for their chili dinner? I know he's already talked to you about it."

"Yes, I told him to plan on me." He smiled at the surprise reflected on both men's faces. It wasn't the first time Mitchell had been invited to a social gathering outside of the club by one of its owners or members, but it was the first one he had accepted. He looked forward to attending, which gave him hope he was working his way past mourning and into acceptance. Tossing back the last swallow of his drink, he nodded toward the back doors where Avery joined Leslie and Kelsey as they came in. "I think your subs need your attention more than my personal life does."

Grayson held out his hand to Avery as she stepped behind the bar, her short, silky sheath clinging to her plump, unfettered breasts and rounded stomach. "They're more fun to torment, that's for sure." With his free hand, he reached up and tweaked a distended nipple before resting his palm on her baby bump.

"Master Mitchell, it's good to see you again." Leslie's blue eyes lit with pleasure as she leaned against Kurt, her damp red camisole and satin boy shorts adhering to her damp curves and drawing his eyes to her long slender legs.

"You too, Leslie. And what's this?" Mitchell lifted a brow as he picked up the blonde's left hand and eyed the large diamond adorning her ring finger. "I didn't know congratulations were in order." A pang gripped him as he wondered if he'd kept himself so aloof his closest friend hadn't thought to inform him of his engagement.

"No one did until tonight. Sorry, Mitchell. You arrived after our big announcement and there hasn't been a chance to bring it up." Kurt sent Leslie a possessive look of love as he slid a hand down the back of her shorts. Both her and Avery's faces glowed in pleasure of their Dom's touch. Mitchell worked to school his features to hide the spasm of emotional pain his friend's good fortune generated.

Cupping Leslie's face, he kissed her before holding out his hand to Kurt. "Congratulations." He tugged on her long hair with a grin. "You've reeled in a good one."

"And Kelsey just accepted Devin and Greg's proposal," Avery announced, drawing their attention to the threesome making their way up the stairs to the loft. Devin held the petite sub they shared over his shoulder and she lifted her dangling, white-haired head to finger wave at them, her ring sparkling from across the space.

"Just so long as it's not a requirement I didn't know about, I'm happy for all of you," Mitchell stated as the memories of his one chance at such happiness played through his head. When the two scenes he'd indulged in with Lillian intruded and kept him from hooking up with anyone before leaving The Barn an hour later, he drove home wondering how he would put her aside like the others with her staying so close.

Salt Lake City

Bryan stood beside Brad's hospital bed, gazing down at his brother's pale face and bandaged head. *Damn stubborn fool.* His hands fisted as he imagined what would have happened if Brad hadn't finally realized he wasn't immune to serious injury and gotten help for what turned out to be a slow brain bleed. Just the sound of it scared Bryan all over again. According to the surgeon who performed the operation a few hours ago, his brother would recover but would require a combination of therapy and drug treatment.

Knowing how close he had come to losing his only sibling, Bryan wasn't in the mood to let the person responsible get by with what she'd done any longer. Brad wouldn't like it, but he planned to go after Lillian Gillespie and bring her back to face a charge of attempted murder. He had no doubt he could make that charge stick if he got hold of and destroyed the pictures she claimed to have of bruises Brad had put on her. He was sure the woman deserved every one given her jealous behavior and the jeopardy she'd put Brad's life in.

Reaching down, he squeezed Brad's shoulder. "I'll be back. Trust me to make this right."

Bryan lit up as soon as he reached the hospital parking lot. He should quit, if for no other reason than to make his brother happy. Brad had been harping on him to get help to kick his chain-smoking habit since the day he started medical school. The truth was, Bryan not only craved the addictive nicotine rush, but he *liked* smoking. It gave him something to do with his hands and calmed him as he dealt with the stress of his job. Working Vice put him in contact with a lot of scum and as far as negative ways to cope, walking around with a lit cigarette in his hand so he could relish the burn of pungent smoke filling his lungs whenever he wanted wasn't near as bad as the lines his cop friends crossed. At least he hadn't sunk so low as to accept a bribe or line his pockets from a bust before turning in evidence.

As Bryan drove away from the hospital and his suffering brother, he realized what he was planning would cross over those lines he'd been so proud of avoiding since making detective ten years ago. Tracking down Lillian's whereabouts by tracing her finances would be on the up and up using resources at the precinct, but he didn't doubt ridding her of those pictures would require breaking a few laws. As he recalled Brad's slurred speech, loss of physical coordination and almost daily nausea that had laid him low since she'd attacked him, he didn't feel in the least guilty for what he planned to do.

Getting retribution for the pain and suffering she'd caused his little brother was all that concerned Bryan right now, that and Brad gaining full recovery of his life and health.

Chapter 7

Lillian kept the 9:00 a.m. appointment at the clinic Monday morning, swearing that wasn't disappointment tugging at her when another doctor called her in to tell her the x-rays a tech had taken were clear. After checking her for lingering tenderness and giving her instructions not to overdo for another week, she walked out of the clinic promising herself not to give Mitchell another thought. The man was good at giving her orgasms and irritating her, and that was it.

Unlike most years in Utah, March was not rolling in like a lion here in Montana. This week's temperatures were expected to reach the lower fifties, prompting Lillian to zip up her coat and walk the one block over to the town square as she left the clinic. It was still cold enough her breath blew out in white puffs, but the bright mid-morning sun was already warm enough to make the air tolerable.

The walk helped calm her irrational disgruntlement over not getting Mitchell's personal attention at the clinic. He never said the appointment would be with him, she admitted, and since he annoyed her when he wasn't touching her naked body, she couldn't understand why her mood had taken a nose-dive after he'd pawned her off on his colleague.

Coming around the corner into the square, Lillian stopped in her tracks upon seeing a large moose with broad antlers meandering across the cobblestone courtyard as if he didn't have a care in the world. Even several feet away, the animal's size was intimidating. As she stood there pondering the safety of going around the buck, Gertie stepped out of the diner and moved in front of her.

"Just stand still, girl. They're harmless, for the most part, but if startled, they can move fast and attack. Big son-of-a-bitch, isn't he?"

"Yes, and he doesn't look to be in a hurry to leave here. The one that ran out in front of me a few weeks ago was smaller and didn't have those antlers, yet still managed to scare the crap out of me."

Gertie snorted. "City girl. That would have been a female. This guy might linger for a while. May as well come in for a cup of coffee and piece of pie. All I have is chocolate cream."

She opened the door and went back inside the diner, expecting, Lillian was sure, for her to follow. Who needed Mitchell's friendship when people like Gertie were so nice to her? A giggle worked its way up her throat as she entered the restaurant imagining the gruff woman's reaction if someone called her nice. She stayed for an hour, eating pie and talking to friendly patrons who took the time to chat for a few minutes, before strolling down to the library after the moose finally lumbered off. Willa greeted her with a wave and held up a book as Lillian approached the counter.

"I saved this back for you, figuring you would be in soon. It's a new release I think you'll like if you don't already have it."

"Oh, no, I don't and I saw this advertised. Thank you so much." She pulled the book she finished from her bag and traded it for the new thriller, the librarian's consideration warming her as much as Gertie's brusque invitation for coffee and pie.

Leaving the library, Lillian veered toward Nan's teashop and ran right into Grayson Monroe as he exited the city building. "Oops, sorry, Sheriff," she apologized, stepping back. She only got a glimpse of his eyes from under his lowered Stetson, but it was enough to see the same probing intensity Mitchell would look at her with that always put her on guard. Or maybe it was the size of the men in Montana that caused her to take notice with more interest than she'd ever bestowed toward anyone back home.

"Lillian. You look better than the last time I saw you."

"I feel much better," she returned, relaxing. "I've met Avery. Your first?"

He nudged his hat back and smiled around the toothpick. "Yes, a girl." He looked around at the parked cars. "Where are you parked?"

"I walked over from the clinic. I'm headed to the teashop now, so I won't keep you." She made to go around him but he reached out and touched her arm, a hard glint entering his eyes.

"If you give me his name, I can contact the authorities in Salt Lake City, make sure he won't come after you."

Lillian thought of Bryan, Brad's cop brother, and how he'd covered for Brad's bad behavior, doubting anyone Grayson talked to would take him seriously. As long as she kept hold of those pictures, she didn't worry about Brad trying to track her down. "Thank you but that's not necessary. He's not a problem anymore. Have a good day, Sheriff."

"You too."

Awareness of his eyes following her all the way to the teashop rippled down her spine, but instead of getting under her skin, the same pleasant rush she'd experienced with Gertie and Willa's thoughtfulness washed through her. An older man she didn't recognize waved to her from across the courtyard as she reached Nan's teashop. She returned the friendly gesture thinking Liana would have liked this small town. Her sister had been more of a homebody than Lillian, preferring takeout and movie rentals to dining in public or going to a theater. But she could see her enjoying the laid-back atmosphere and people at Dale's Diner and spending an evening at the small cinema housed in what appeared to be the original, decades old theater. With a tight clutch around her heart, she remembered how Liana would compromise whenever Lillian insisted they try a new place to eat or view a certain film on the big screen. Their mother always said Liana was much better at give and take than Lillian.

God, I miss you, sis. Sucking in a deep breath to ward off the encroaching melancholy, she stuck her head inside the teashop, spotting Nan wiping down the table closest to the door.

"Hi there. I just wanted to accept that offer of a ride out to the barbeque, if you're sure they want me."

Nan nodded without hesitation as she lifted the small tray holding empty cups and plates. "I'm sure. Sydney called first thing this morning double checking the head count and is looking forward to meeting you. Do you have time to come in?"

"No, sorry. I've been out all morning and want to paint while the sun is still coming through the window at the apartment."

"Catch you later then."

Much to Lillian's annoyance, Mitchell's bothersome step back from doctoring her himself wasn't enough to deter her from continuing to watch for him first thing in the mornings over the next few days. As much as she wanted to, she couldn't stop thinking about the 'lesson' he'd heaped upon her butt or prevent the memory of her response to those slaps from becoming fantasies flitting through her mind as her traitorous body heated eyeing his tall, loose-limbed stride out to his vehicle. By Friday, she was forced to admit she lusted after the damn man despite his dominant nature going against everything she'd ever thought she wanted, or didn't want, in a man.

Maybe it's time to move on, she considered as she saw an SUV pull into the drive and disappointment gripped her throat when she realized it wasn't Mitchell but Nan's husband arriving to pick Lillian up. She wondered if Mitchell would be at the Dunbar's tonight, was working late or had gone to his club without coming home first, and then wanted to kick herself for thinking about him. *Gratitude for being there for me that night at his cabin, that's all this obsession is.* That's what she'd been telling herself lately, disregarding the thirty minutes he had tormented her over his lap a week ago and she'd exploded from the pain-driven pleasure.

Snatching her coat, she skipped down the stairs, looking forward to the evening.

Twenty minutes later, Dan parked behind a row of several other vehicles in the circular drive in front of a sprawling ranch home and Lillian got her first look at a working ranch. A herd of black cattle foraged for dried grass in the pasture behind the barns and beyond them, the Dunbar land stretched as far as the eye could see. Snow still blanketed over half of the prairie and the artist in her craved to see the landscape strewn with spring foliage.

The ride down the long narrow road leading up to the house and other structures was a lot bumpier than the snow-cleared highway they'd taken when leaving Willow Springs. Lillian slid out of the back seat with the urge to rub her butt, but considering what she'd heard about the men she was about to meet, not to mention Nan's husband, she didn't think that was a good idea.

"You look nervous," Nan pointed out as the three of them reached the front door.

Lillian flicked a glance up at Dan before saying, "I'm hoping I don't stick out like a sore thumb tonight since I'll be the only one who isn't a member of that club."

"You won't," Dan assured her, placing a hand on her back as he opened the door.

She wanted to argue how he could be so sure and then let it go as she remembered the futility of questioning Mitchell after he would utter such an assertive comment. Entering the warm house, a pair of collies bounded up to her, tails wagging in greeting, followed by a smiling, pregnant red head with bright green eyes.

"You're Lillian. Thanks so much for coming. I'm Sydney and

this is Spike and Sadie." Sydney reached down to stroke Spike's black head.

Lillian returned her smile as she scratched Sadie behind the ears. "Nice to meet you, and these two."

"Dan, the guys are in the den." Sydney beckoned Nan and Lillian to follow her. "Avery and Tamara are in the kitchen with me."

Following her host and the tantalizing aroma, Lillian caught a glimpse of several men gathered around a corner bar in a massive great room and recognized the back of Mitchell's salt and pepper head. She shouldn't feel so relieved at seeing he was here and not at his club, especially after the way he'd pawned her off on another doctor. Squaring her shoulders, she looked away and hardened her resolve to stay immune to his presence.

"You have a beautiful home," she told Sydney as they entered a kitchen with every modern convenience, her mouth watering at the pan of homemade biscuits another heavily pregnant woman was sliding out of the oven.

"Thank you. Tamara, this is Doc's Lillian." Sydney flicked her a teasing grin as Lillian shook her head.

"No, I'm not. There's nothing between us. Nice to meet you, Tamara."

Tamara laughed and took the bottle of wine Lillian handed her. "You sound just like Connor a year ago. I swear, if that man had denied what was obvious to everyone else one more time, I would have washed my hands of him. Thanks for this." She grabbed an opener off the counter. "I'll pour for you and Nan."

Avery smirked at Tamara as she handed her a glass of juice. "No, you wouldn't have, and you know it. You might have smacked some sense into him, but you would have hung in there. Besides, once he caved to the inevitable, he's hardly let you out of his sight for long."

Tamara's gray eyes shone with pleasure as she released an exaggerated dreamy sigh. "Yeah, I know."

Sydney moved to the stove to stir the big pot of bubbling chili that was responsible for the aroma tickling Lillian's senses as soon as she'd entered the house. Turning her head, she said, "Just you and Master Mitchell, alone for almost three days and then he invites you to stay in his spare room and there's nothing between you? Are you sure you're female?"

The others giggled and Lillian had to smile and admit Sydney had her there. Despite the doctor's dominant personality waving red flags of undesirability, she'd failed to stay indifferent to him. Unlike at the cabin, there were no excuses for caving to his high-handedness in the apartment, or a reason for her uncharacteristic response other than she *was* female and he was so freaking male.

Because they had been so welcoming and friendly toward her, she felt she owed them the truth, or a small part of it. "Okay, but it's not what you think. Nan mentioned he's a member of your club, and I respect that's a big part of your relationships, but those proclivities have never held an interest for me. Mitchell was nice at the cabin. I was in the first days of grieving for my sister and he helped me through a bad night. It didn't mean anything beyond that, and neither did his offer to stay in the room above his garage while I'm here, since I'm just passing through."

"One thing about dominant men, they tend to jump into protective mode and are damn good at helping when we're going through a rough time. I'm glad Mitchell was there for you. Dealing with your sister's death and your ex's abuse must still haunt you, so I hope you won't get in a hurry to leave," Nan said, pouring herself a refill and leaning against the counter.

Tamara nodded. "What Nan said. We're just teasing you, and we've all been in denial over the perks from the lifestyle when we first explored it, so don't dismiss it out of hand just yet."

Lillian wasn't sure how to reply to either of them. She appreciated the request for her to stick around, but the suggestion she might reserve judgment on whether she was interested in exploring their sexual preferences had never entered her mind. "I don't go for the bossy type," she stated, opting for blunt honesty.

"I didn't think I did either, until Master Grayson helped me one night, his voice and commands alone sucking me in enough I tracked him down here to enlist his help and see if my response that one time was due to stress, a fluke or the real thing." Avery rested a hand on her rounded stomach. "And I've never regretted taking that chance."

A tightness spread around Lillian's chest and coiled in her abdomen as she eyed the contented faces of these women. There was no denying they were happy with their spouses, and that included the alternative sex they indulged in, yet each one appeared to maintain their independence, working in their chosen careers and running their homes without dictation from their 'Dom' spouses. Surely it was envy of that special connection with someone that she once cherished with Liana she was experiencing, and not a yearning for a relationship such as theirs.

Before she could come up with anything to say, a deep voice drew the dogs' attention toward the door.

"Spike, Sadie, go lie down."

Lillian looked up at the man entering the kitchen, his enigmatic blue eyes zeroing in on Sydney with a possessive glint. *Wow*, was all she could think as he turned toward her and held out a large, calloused hand in greeting.

"You must be Lillian. I'm Caden. Welcome to our home."

"Thank you." His hand engulfed hers in a gentle grip but it was the man leading the others toward the kitchen who snagged her attention.

With the strong pull of a magnet, her gaze was drawn behind her host, toward Mitchell, who regarded her with a bland expression. He appeared relaxed holding a drink, those broad shoulders stretching his casual knit pullover.

Despite his neutral look, her pulse jumped, like always. With several eyes focused on them, she managed to throttle down the now familiar response, refusing to cave to this weird attraction again, especially after he'd dropped her as his patient.

"I'm glad Mitchell was around to help you out when that

snowstorm struck. That one even caught us unaware," Caden said as the men filed into the kitchen.

Shifting out of their way, Lillian sighed with a rueful grin, flicking Mitchell a questioning glance as she wondered how much he had told his friends. "I missed the turnoff for Billings, which is where I'd planned to stop for the night, and am grateful for the doctor's hospitality."

"It was no problem," Mitchell interjected smoothly before turning toward Sydney. "Sydney, are you going to make us smell that much longer without feeding us?"

"Nope. It's ready. Buffet style, so get in line and load up."

To Lillian's surprise, Mitchell moved to stand to the side with her as everyone filed in. "I didn't know you were coming tonight or I would have offered you a ride."

She brought her glass of wine to her mouth and sipped as she flicked her eyes up at him. Forcing a cool tone, she let her disgruntlement with him win out over self-preservation to keep her feelings to herself. "I find that hard to believe since you couldn't bother telling me yourself about the x-rays you insisted I have taken."

Before he could answer, a tall man sporting a sexy, bristled jaw and eyes as blue as Caden's stopped in front of them. "Nice to meet you, Lillian. I'm Connor, Caden's brother and this one's lord and master." He yanked Tamara against his side with a teasing grin.

"Ha, you like to think so, don't you? Don't listen to a word he says, Lillian."

Grinning, she shook Connor's hand, not surprised Tamara had refused to give up on this man. What would it be like to spend years of your childhood with such a protective, close friend looking out for you and then reap the rewards of that special relationship growing into such a deep caring commitment? Sadness tugged at Lillian as she thought of the bond she and Liana had shared since birth, and the void her passing left that would always be with her.

"Everyone ignores Connor's teasing." Mitchell clasped her elbow and steered her toward the dwindling food line, confusing her with his continued attention. "You're getting between me and food, Dunbar."

"Got it." Connor winked at Lillian and she forced the encroaching sorrow back before it could ruin the evening.

After getting their food, everyone filed into the dining room where Mitchell surprised her again by taking the seat next to her. She cast him a disapproving look, his nearness making it difficult for her to suppress the unaccustomed ache to be a part of this close-knit group instead of an outsider. *It's just because I miss Liana, not because I have anything in common with any of them.* That was the only explanation she could come up with for the growing desire to stick around Willow Springs and get to know these people better.

Mitchell ignored her silent reproach, turning his attention to his food and the conversations going on around the table. Since she couldn't figure out what was going on with him, she dug into the best chili she'd ever tasted, Sydney's concoction outdoing the quick, simple pot she had thrown together at the cabin.

"What did you do different, Sydney?" Grayson took another bite, frowning as he tried to place the unique flavor. "This is good."

Relief spread across Sydney's face as she inched one hand under the table. "I'm glad you like it. I took a chance on trying a new recipe I saw on the Food Network, adding pork and pumpkin."

"Sydney."

Caden glared at his wife and she tossed him an innocent smile as she brought her hand up from under the table. Since Lillian felt the brush of both dogs against her legs, she guessed Caden disapproved of the pieces of cheese Sydney had snuck them.

"What?" She batted her eyes at her husband but it was clear he wasn't fooled.

A few chuckled at their cook's sweet smile before Connor sent his brother an amused grin. "You may as well give up, bro. How many rescues do you have now?"

"Not as many since Matilda died." Sydney blinked back tears.

"Matilda was an old mule we brought back from auction last fall. She had more health issues than we thought," Caden told Lillian as he squeezed Sydney's hand, his rugged features softening as he ran his thumb over her knuckles.

"That's too bad," she murmured, her heart turning over.

Not so much for the poor animal, but for herself. The teasing comradery going on around the table coupled with the possessive, sometimes carnal looks the men sent their significant others, kept emphasizing how alone she was in the world now, and how much she missed Liana. She'd been more than her sister; she was her best friend and they were as close as these girls appeared. Not to mention the men who had come and gone in her life without leaving a lasting impression who'd never looked at her with a fraction of the caring and lust these guys weren't shy about revealing.

Fighting back the encroaching despondency, she finished the meal listening more than conversing and then stood with Sydney and the other girls to collect the dishes. Her eyes clashed with Mitchell's potent gaze as she reached for his empty bowl. After ignoring him for the last thirty minutes, the jolt from that look zapped her from head to toe in a lightning bolt of heat, catching her off guard. She shied away from acknowledging a flicker of awareness hinting at something other than simple lust.

"Excuse me," she murmured. He circled her wrist, her heart pounding harder just from the swipe of his thumb across her pulse.

"Drive back with me."

The way he tended to order instead of ask never failed to rub Lillian wrong, but at least it distracted her from the sensations his caressing thumb had triggered. Before she could reply, he added one word that was so unexpected, she found herself powerless to resist.

"Please."

Lillian followed Sydney into the kitchen without answering and Mitchell struggled with the urge to go all Dom on her in front of everyone and insist she accept his offer. His uncharacteristic interest in her despite how unsuited she was for his preferences continued to plague him; the step away from being her doctor proving to have no effect on throttling back a desire he couldn't label and was losing the battle fighting.

Tonight, it was that same spasm of sorrow crossing her face he had glimpsed at the cabin that crumbled his will to keep her at arm's length. The downward turn of her lips accompanied a sheen in her purple eyes that gave away her thoughts, and her grief. Telling himself it was just his own experience with loss and bereavement that kept drawing him to her was no longer working and it was time he explored other ways to put an end to whatever this was.

"What's up, Doc?"

Mitchell cut his gaze from watching Lillian's shapely ass encased in snug denim toward Connor's amused voice. He knew better than to ask the younger Dunbar what he meant. "Just trying to save Dan a trip back into town."

"We planned on having Lillian overnight," Dan said, defusing Mitchell's excuse with a small smirk that matched Connor's.

The problem with getting close to people again was they got to know you well, sometimes too well. "Forget it, you two. It's just an offer of a ride, nothing more." He didn't include Caden or Grayson in his rebuke as both remained silent. "She's at her easel working first thing in the morning, I'm guessing to take advantage of the natural sunlight. You're not going to want to get up early to bring her back into town."

Mitchell had spotted Lillian sitting at the window as he'd left the house for work each morning this past week, but doubted she'd paid attention. Even though he'd made sure he wasn't obvious about checking on her, he could tell she'd been absorbed in her craft. Until he figured out what it was that kept this one woman in the forefront of his thoughts and how to handle his unwanted preoccupation, he refused to let anyone believe there was anything starting between them.

The good thing about having close friends was they knew when to back off. Dan nodded and stood. "Whatever she wants to do is fine."

"I'll go check with her. Thanks." Rising, he strode toward the kitchen, halting before entering as he heard the invitation Nan was issuing to Lillian.

"Come on, Lillian. What have you got to lose? You can come as our guest to socialize. There's no rule stating you have to participate in a scene. Now that the guys have renovated the west side loft into three private rooms, we have several members who prefer private scenes, and some who come just to watch."

He recognized Avery's voice as she added her encouragement. "I was trying to learn as much about Grayson as I could before enlisting his help when I went the first time. It's definitely something you have to experience firsthand before you'll know if it's your thing. You're not out anything by appeasing your curiosity."

"And," Sydney piped in, "I can verify watching our doctor in Dom mode is time worth spending. If you're still planning on leaving soon, what have you got to lose?"

"You're very persuasive, so I'll think about it."

Every muscle in Mitchell's body tightened upon hearing Lillian's soft reply. It was way too easy to recall her hold on the fireplace mantle at his insistence and her response to his hands, including when he had added a touch of discomfort to the budding pleasure. He'd increased that painful stimulation as she lay over his lap last week, and his dreams were still disturbed by the way she lifted her lush ass for his swats and her strident cries as she'd splintered apart. He doubted he could keep her at arm's length at the club as he imagined her expression viewing some of the scenes. She wouldn't judge or condemn, her quick friendship and acceptance of the girls was proof of that, but she would continue to deny she possessed any interest or an ounce of submissiveness. It might be best if he talked her out of going.

Pivoting, he walked to the entry and retrieved their coats as he contemplated the clutch in his gut when Sydney mentioned Lillian leaving soon, along with what to do if she agreed to an evening at the club. Something else he needed to give some serious thought to.

She entered the foyer as he started back toward the kitchen, eyeing her coat over his arm with a sardonic look that caused his palm to itch in reply. "I don't recall agreeing to your offer."

"So you want to put your friends out by asking them to take you home first thing in the morning?"

"Nan opens the tea shop by seven, so it won't be an imposition," she returned as smoothly as Mitchell realized Dan had set him up. "But I've already told her I'll go back with you."

"Then, if you're ready, let's go." Holding out her coat, he didn't ask why as the others filed into the entry on their way out.

Lillian couldn't help it, the desire to spend time with Mitchell outweighed her determination to forget him following his desertion as her doctor. When all she could think about was her reaction every time he leveled that focused gaze on her after Nan invited her to visit their club, she decided to give in to his offer and work towards getting him out of her system. It wouldn't do for her to leave in a week or two and still have these mind-consuming, libido stirring thoughts about a man she wouldn't see again.

Once they hit the highway, they limited their conversation to the evening until they reached Willow Springs and then he surprised her with his abrupt change of subject. "Are you considering visiting The Barn tomorrow night?"

His deep tone washed through her with its usual warmth, another reason she needed to do whatever was necessary to end this odd infatuation. "You heard that, huh?"

"Yes. And given your constant gripes about bossy men, I'm wondering why you would consider it."

She sent him a teasing grin as he turned on his street. "How do you know it's not just your high-handedness I've complained about?"

"Is it?" he returned with cool insistence.

Sighing, she admitted, "No. It's not my thing, but I am curious."

Pulling into the drive, he swung toward her as he cut the engine. "I didn't prove you wrong about that last week?"

He would have to remind her of *that*. She wouldn't deny what had been so obvious, but neither would she admit that meant she would enjoy a regular dose of his kinks. Instead, she planted another seed by saying, "Who knows? Maybe I'll discover I get off on voyeurism. Goodnight, Doc. Thanks for the lift."

Lillian's hopes of getting away with having the last word were dashed when she'd no sooner gotten out of the vehicle and he was there, pinning her against the door with his towering, ripped body pressed against hers. She went hot, her heart rate tripping even as irritation over his domination rippled under her skin.

Before she could tell him to back off, he bent his head and nipped at her chin and then took her lower lip between his teeth and bit. The sharp sting ricocheted straight down to her pussy in an undeniable heated gush. Swallowing back a moan, she gripped his biceps and demanded in a hoarse voice, "What are you playing at, Mitchell?"

"Not playing, proving a point." Gripping her shoulders, he spun her around and placed her hands on the hood of the SUV.

"I don't care for your caveman tactics," she stated, proud of her scornful, rigid tone despite her quivering muscles as he worked his hands inside her coat.

"So you say," he returned with the same arrogance lacing his voice. "But your body says otherwise whenever I put my hands on you. Wonder why that is?"

Gripping her nipples, he plucked at the tender buds, and even through her sweater and bra, his pinch and rotation was strong enough to elicit another body quaking response. She wouldn't fight it, or deny it, couldn't if she wanted to get over it and move on.

"Lust is easy to explain," she answered on a deeply indrawn breath.

"Now, there I can agree with you." Mitchell released her nipples and moved back as fast as he'd commanded her senses.

Lowering her hands, she turned and pulled her coat closed. "We can agree on something. Good for us. Goodnight, again."

He waited until she was halfway up the stairs on the side of the garage before he said, "You could have dropped your hands and moved away at any time. If you go tomorrow night and see anything that interests you, let me know. I'll be around."

Gazing down at him, she replied, "What if there is someone else I'd rather have… enlighten me?"

"Better the Dom you know than a stranger, at least the first time."

Lillian eyed his back as he strode toward the house, resisting the urge to stick out her tongue. Why did he have to be so good at countering her taunts with such effective comebacks? He didn't even offer to escort her out to the secluded club, maybe hoping she wouldn't go? Damn, but he irritated her even as he turned her on and left her aching for more of his touch, and just his.

Chapter 8

Bryan looked up as a car passed him and turned the corner onto the street he'd been surveilling since spotting Lillian Gillespie earlier that day and following her to the local doctor's residence. It had been easy to track her whereabouts through credit card and phone records, proving she wasn't overly concerned about or on the run from her assault on Brad. Dumb bitch. As soon as it appeared she'd settled in Podunk, he'd taken vacation time and jumped in his car. After checking into a local motel in Billings, paying cash for a few nights stay, he'd made the drive to Willow Springs every day for three days, checking the places where she'd used her credit card in the hopes of catching sight of her since she hadn't rerouted her mail delivery yet.

Slumping in the seat, he watched the car turn into the doctor's driveway. A flutter of excitement stirred inside him as the light at the top of the steps leading to the room above the garage shone on Lillian's red hair as she emerged. He stayed hidden in the dark corner until they drove off then waited another five minutes before getting out and winding his way behind the neighbors to reach her new residence. Lifting his cigarette to his mouth, he held it there with his lips as he unscrewed the lightbulb and then squatted in front of the door to work the flimsy lock.

Slipping inside, he spotted the computer right away and got to work. The faster he found and deleted those pictures, the sooner he could return with a warrant.

What the hell am I doing, Sis? Lillian had asked herself that question numerous times all day and continued to do so on the way out to this private club. *Am I going tonight to appease my curiosity, to keep from missing you so much or because there's a certain doctor I can't seem to get out of my system, even knowing he's into the whole dominant sexual control thing?* Her sister had always been the one she confided in, the one she could bounce ideas off of, vent to or seek advice from. The acute void from Liana's loss had threatened to drag her down all day as she'd struggled to choose from riding to The Barn with Nan or telling her she'd changed her mind. *What the hey,* she'd thought, using Liana's favorite expression as she dashed out to Nan's car when she honked. *I'll be packing up and leaving anytime now, so why not go and see what the big draw is for these people?* That thought drew a tightness in her chest she refused to think about right now.

"Thanks again for picking me up," Lillian said, running her hands down her black, pleated skirt. "You're sure this is okay?" She waved a hand in front of her white, button-up silk blouse.

"Perfect. You're still covered more than the Masters like, but as a guest you'll be fine. Master Grayson approved your guest pass and a waiver on attire, but like I said this morning, you'll be more comfortable meeting in the middle of the required dress code of short skirts or shorts. Dan went early for a meeting with the Masters, but I can show you around before I meet up with him."

"Okay, that's just weird, needing a waiver on wearing jeans

and a sweater to a club." And she had a feeling that was a minor oddity compared to what she would be viewing soon.

Nan chuckled as she pulled onto the highway. "You remind me of my first visit. The only difference is I already knew I was sexually submissive and was eager to explore my options."

"I already know I'm not, but I'm not a prude. Doesn't everyone fantasize about voyeurism?"

"Probably, but few are brave enough to appease their curiosity. Stay open to other potential turn-ons and you might surprise yourself, or not, considering Master Mitchell has already given you a taste of what he likes."

Two tastes, Lillian reflected, intending to keep that tidbit to herself. She still had trouble reconciling with her easy capitulation of lying over Mitchell's lap for a bare-butt spanking and she wasn't about to give Nan more ammunition to use against her denials of possessing even one submissive bone in her body.

"He caught me at a grief-stricken moment, when my defenses were down."

"And he's an excellent Dom, experienced in knowing what, and how much to control and give. I'll bet you climaxed more than once." Nan smirked as she turned onto a narrow, unpaved road that bisected woodsy trees.

"I was long overdue," Lillian admitted with a rueful smile. "Where the heck is this place?" Other than the headlights illuminating their way, they were enshrouded in darkness.

"Right... here." They emerged into a clearing and Nan whipped into a space between two oversized pickup trucks in the gravel lot as Lillian took in the huge renovated barn.

Following Nan across the lot, she resisted the urge to look for Mitchell's SUV. "A lot of work went into this place," she said as they stepped through the wide double doors into a spacious foyer.

"Yes, it did, and they keep adding changes. Shoes off and in one of these cubbies." Nan toed off her ankle boots and Lillian followed suit, assuming this was one of those weird rules that went with the required shorts, skirts or anything else that left a lot of bare skin showing. Shrugging out of her knee-length coat, Nan asked with a wicked grin, "Ready, girlfriend?"

Eying her friend's black lace corset that showcased and revealed her full breasts and the matching thong, she already felt out of place before even entering the club. "As I'll ever be."

"Relax, you'll have fun no matter how far you go tonight."

Instant denial sprang to her lips. "I'm only… *holy shit.*" Stopping dead in her tracks as soon as she entered the main club space, strident cries echoing down from her upper left drew Lillian's eyes. The lighting was dimmer in the open loft but she could still make out the naked woman whose arms and legs were stretched in wide V's, bound to what appeared to be a wooden X frame. A few feet from that contraption, another woman's wrists were cuffed to a dangling chain and two men held her between them, their tandem thrusting in and out of the petite blonde's pussy and ass the most erotic thing Lillian had ever witnessed. The pose, with the men's heads bent to each side of her arched neck, their hands roaming in soothing caresses as they used her body with care, kept her gaze riveted on the threesome.

"That's Kelsey and Masters Greg and Devin. The guys broke the news of their relationship to their families last Christmas and got their support and blessings to marry. Now they have to decide which man will be her legal husband."

Tearing her eyes away from the scene, Lillian followed Nan toward the circular bar in the center of the lower floor, winding through the tables and chairs on the way. From that brief observation of the trio, she didn't envy their decision. Her steps faltered as she spotted Mitchell at the bar the moment he scowled at something a young, pretty blonde said to both him and the black-haired, black-eyed bartender as she trailed her fingers down Mitchell's rigid arm with a coy smile. In a quick move, he pinned her hands behind her back and pressed her torso down on the bar top. The three hard smacks he delivered on her wriggling, silk panty-covered butt caused Lillian's cheeks to clench in remembered pleasure/pain.

Mitchell pulled her up and the chastised girl lowered her eyes, saying something to the bartender that seemed to appease both men. Lillian couldn't help it, she rolled her eyes, put off by the girl's subdued posture and the pleasure reflected on her face as both men nodded their approval. Naturally, Mitchell would have to swing his observant gaze her way at that precise moment. One dark brow winged up as he eyed her with cool reproach.

Nan sighed next to her. "If that look doesn't make you shiver, there's something seriously wrong with you, girlfriend."

"You go for that heavy handedness, I don't. It's just a difference in preferences," Lillian returned, her heart thumping faster as Mitchell slid off the bar stool and strolled toward her.

"Uh, huh. And how many orgasms did you say he gave you?"

"Shut up."

Nan laughed and then turned her smile on Mitchell with a devious gleam in her eyes. "Master Mitchell. I think you could give Lillian a better tour and insight into our lifestyle than me. Do you mind?"

"Not at all. I can start with explaining the necessity of showing respect, not only to us Doms, but the submissives who don't hide from or deny their needs."

Disapproval colored his deep tenor and that shiver Nan mentioned rippled under Lillian's skin, his chastisement hitting its mark. He was right. She didn't understand the draw of dominance but could have sworn she didn't judge. It wasn't pleasant discovering a new flaw in her character.

"She seems young to know this is what she wants," Lillian said in defense, watching the girl bounce off with another man as if nothing unfavorable had just happened.

Mitchell grasped her elbow, as if to ensure she didn't take off, and nodded at Nan. "I'll take good care of our guest, Nan. Thank you."

"Have fun, Lillian."

It was hard, but Lillian resisted the urge to stick her tongue out at her friend's smug face before Nan pivoted and went to join Avery and another woman at their table.

"Good call," Mitchell murmured with a twitch of his lips.

"What? Are you a mind reader, too?" she snapped, not sure why she was annoyed.

"No, just getting good at reading your expressions. Would you like to dance or get a drink before I show you around upstairs?"

A drink sounded good, a double even better, but didn't think that request would go over well here. "I'll take a scotch on the rocks, but I have to get my wallet out of the foyer."

"No need." Steering her toward the bar, he grasped her waist and lifted her onto a stool. "Two drinks are part of your guest pass, or membership if you join."

She frowned, refraining from chiding him over the assistance she didn't need or ask for. "Why would I join if I'm leaving soon?" And why did voicing the truth produce a constriction in her chest she couldn't explain?

"Just saying. Master Kurt, this is Lillian, our guest tonight and she'd like a scotch on the rocks," Mitchell told the bartender.

Master Kurt's mouth curled in a smile that softened his dark, five-o'clock shadowed face and ink-dark eyes. "Feel the need for a strong nerve booster, do you?"

Lillian shrugged. "I admit to being green about all this," she waved her arm, indicating the room at large, "so, yeah, a good punch to the system wouldn't hurt."

Kurt nodded, the approval stamped on his face giving her a jolt of pleasure. Another one of those responses that perplexed her.

"Mitchell, are you ready for another beer?"

"I'll hold off for now. We're headed upstairs for a tour and a few ground rules."

Both of them smirked as she unintentionally scowled at the word 'rules'. "What?" she groused.

"Not one for rules?" Kurt asked.

"As Mitchell knows, I'm not one for bossy men. I understand rules are necessary."

"Ah, that's what that look was for. I'll get your drink."

Mitchell placed two fingers under her chin and drew her head up to face him. "Good. You're required to show a modicum of respect to all the Masters, but I'll give you a pass on addressing me as Master Mitchell, or Sir for tonight. If you return, remember that."

Since she didn't think that was likely, she agreed and let it go. "Is he a good friend of yours?" She glanced at Kurt, or rather, *Master* Kurt.

A contemplative look crossed his face as he shifted his gaze toward the bartender. "He returned to his family ranch for good after living a few years in Texas about the same time I moved to Willow Springs. We met when his father suffered a stroke, so, yeah, I know him best out of everyone else. I'm stabling my horse out at his place, so I try to get out there once a week."

Tonight, dressed in tight denim, cowboy boots and a black tee shirt that emphasized his broad shoulders, thick biceps and six-pack abs, she could easily picture him astride a horse with his Stetson pulled low. She could just as easily recall the vision of him naked and the proof his lean build was made of sinewy muscles that drew the eye as he walked.

"The last time I rode was at girl scout camp. Liana and I," she paused to swallow down the lump rising to her throat, "we were ten, I think, and the horses were on the smaller size. It was fun."

He reached for her but she drew back, afraid a conciliatory touch or word would shake her even more. Kurt returned with her drink and she welcomed the distraction.

"Thank you." Sipping the liquor, she relished the fortifying burn down her throat as Mitchell cupped her elbow again and addressed his friend.

"I'll be back to introduce Lillian to Leslie, if you're still manning the bar."

Kurt nodded. "I'm on for another hour. Nice to meet you, Lillian."

"You too." Gripping her glass, she slid off the stool at Mitchell's tug, ignoring the flutter of unease in her stomach as he led her toward the stairs leading to the loft where she'd seen the apparatus coming in. All she could see of the upper level on the other side of the barn were three closed doors.

Pausing at the foot of the stairs, he asked, "Are you ready for a tour, or would you rather stay down here longer?"

Putting it off would only delay proving she was right, that this whole scene wasn't her thing. "No, I'm ready. I came tonight to satisfy my curiosity. I'm sure it won't be more shocking than what's been flitting through my imagination."

"Let's see."

Okay, maybe I spoke too soon, Lillian thought as they reached the top floor and her eyes landed on a webbed swing in the corner. The dim lighting didn't allow for a clear view of Nan's displayed crotch even though her raised legs were cuffed above her head in a wide vee. Dan stood at her side, a fierce look of concentration on his face as he flicked a multi-strand flogger directly on her sensitive, bare flesh. There was no mistaking the rapture spreading over her friend's face, or Lillian's confusion at her response to both the humiliating pose and what must have been blistering pain.

Mitchell gripped her chin and pulled her head around, holding her there as he said, "That's her thing, and her Master's. Some enjoy that extra bite, a few a more rigid, rule-structured approach. Most members in this club concentrate on the physical aspect. None of this is wrong."

Standing in bare feet brought Lillian's head only up to his chest and the way he held her head arched back emphasized his towering height. She didn't care for the intimidating tactic or his cool tone insinuating she was silently judging the couple. "You misinterpreted confusion with distaste. Let me go." To her surprise, he released her chin immediately and stepped back, a closed expression on his face. A wave of disappointment swamped her, whether from the loss of his nearness and touch or that unreadable look, she couldn't figure out, adding to the jumbled chaos of her thoughts.

Lillian shifted her eyes away from Mitchell's ever observant gaze in time to witness Dan snapping those leather strips on Nan's tender flesh again. His other hand had scooped out one breast, and whatever he did to her nipple coincided with that strike, causing his wife to jerk her arms and legs against the restraints and lift her hips with a supplicant cry. Watching Dan's face soften with approval and love elicited a stab of envy she wasn't prepared to deal with.

"Come on, pet. Let's see what you think of a few other scenes."

Mitchell's use of that epithet defused the effect of the warmth lacing his gruff voice and she let him hear her irritation. "You know I don't care for that label."

"Yes, I do. The club safe word is red, but a lot of times a submissive will prefer choosing her own, something she can relate to and remember easily." He stopped by a large wagon wheel suspended from the roof, a much smaller version propped next to it. "We call this apparatus our Wheel of Misfortune." Giving the small one a spin, Lillian watched the little flapper snapping between the spokes until it came to rest on one as it stopped spinning. Mitchell leaned forward and read, "Back to wheel, sideways position. Can you picture yourself up there, strapped on naked, in that position?"

"No." She didn't have to think about it. Not only did it sound uncomfortable, but mortifying.

"Then we'll move on. Tell me when you see something you wouldn't adamantly oppose trying."

"And if there's nothing?"

He shrugged, as if he didn't care one way or the other, the

move producing another stab of unexplainable regret. "Then you've appeased your curiosity and can set it aside."

They walked slowly down the center of the loft, Mitchell pausing to explain each piece of equipment. He pointed out Master Devin, leaning against the back wall, and explained he was on monitoring duty, which entailed keeping an eye out for anyone breaking the safe, sane and consensual rules. Lillian wasn't ready to admit it out loud, but every time she saw unabashed pleasure on a submissive's face, regardless of the torment her Dom was heaping upon her body, and his approval of her acceptance, her curiosity and the slow spread of heat increased. She was starting to get a grip of what her friends meant when they said the lifestyle met their needs.

Lillian couldn't help leaning on Mitchell each time they stopped, the brush of his leg against hers, his firm hold on her arm and deep voice vibrating above her all worked to set her at ease while she reconciled with her arousing response. She quit wondering how her nipples could peak and her pussy swell and dampen when he annoyed her with his commands and continued to use that 'pet' name, but by the time they reached another woman bound to a dangling chain, her body was ablaze with a fiery need she couldn't disclaim, admitting only some of it was due to the erotic displays. It was more proof she didn't require to confess the 'spanking' lesson last week failed to work him out of her system.

Were all these men tall, dark and muscled? Lillian wondered, watching wide-eyed as this Dom wielded a long-stranded flogger with steady, constant flicks of his wrist, moving from the bound woman's buttocks to her thighs then up to her lower back. Her acceptance of the reddening, hurtful swats baffled Lillian – she could still too easily recall the breath-stealing, excruciating pain of Brad's fist and kick.

And then Lillian watched as her eyes glazed, her face softened into a rapt, contented expression, as if she'd drifted into another world. What would it be like to be taken to another plane, outside of yourself, away from everything stressful and hurtful and have a man look at her with the same warm approval etched on this Dom's face? She glanced up at Mitchell as he led her away from the scene, almost stumbling as she realized that's exactly what he had done every time he'd brought her to orgasm. He'd taken her outside of herself, given her a reprieve from grief through seduction at the cabin and the more light-hearted yet just as intense scene – at least for her – at the apartment.

She questioned the quick stab of longing for a similar look of approval from Mitchell that took her by surprise, a reaction she didn't want but admitting it and then moving on seemed more productive than denial. His penchant for issuing orders pushed her buttons but she owed him for looking after her in more ways than one. Maybe someday she would find a way to pay him back.

"Come meet one of my favorite couples," Mitchell said, steering her toward the last apparatus.

She couldn't help it, her jaw dropped as they approached what looked like a gymnastics vault, the contraption rocking back and forth as the naked woman astride it gyrated up and down on a condom-covered, vibrating dildo. Her Dom, a stern looking man in his fifties, flicked the long narrow handle in his hand, snapping the square leather flap at the end on the blonde's already blood-red nipple.

Mitchell pushed her jaw up, closing her gaping mouth as he leaned down to whisper, "They live a strict, twenty-four seven, Dom/sub lifestyle. Do not speak unless one of us gives you permission."

As usual, Lillian bristled at the order, the tight squeeze on her elbow signaling he was dead serious. Swallowing the retort on the tip of her tongue, she nodded, amazed at the woman's ability to maneuver up and down on the fake phallus using just her legs since her hands were cuffed behind her. She gasped as the man swatted the tender flesh of her bare folds clinging to the dildo, lifting her head to reveal wide blue eyes glistening with tears.

"Head down!" the Dom barked and she dropped her head again, her hair falling forward to shield her face.

Lillian's fiercely held independent side rebelled against the woman's subjugated pose and obedience, but Mitchell's sharp, negative head shake kept her mouth shut. And then the man stepped forward, stopped the rocking motion of the machine, rooted out her swollen clit and pressed the sensitive nerve endings against the hard ridges of the vibrator with one word.

"Now."

Climaxing as instructed, the woman's whole body bowed with pleasure, her soft cries resonating around them. As erotically titillating as watching her was, it was the look the two of them shared as the woman opened her eyes, her perspiration-damp body still quivering, her face suffused with pleasure. Lillian couldn't glance away from the obvious special connection the couple shared, the depth of their unguarded feelings exposed in their gazes for all to see. That closeness reminded her of the bond between her and Liana; different relationships for sure, but the same link that made them so unique.

Grief clogged her throat, forcing her to look away from the couple as he helped her down, his hands gentle on her red-marked body. Lillian's eyes rose to catch a fleeting look of sadness and longing in Mitchell's gaze as he looked at his friends, and she suspected he was remembering his wife. She didn't doubt theirs had been as close a bond as this couple. Somehow, realizing how deeply his loss had affected him and his life, made her feel better about being with him now. They both were in need of healing before they could move on.

His eyes swung toward her, the shadow of heartbreak disappearing with a flare that turned them more green than brown. Her heart rolled over, her body quivering as if he'd touched her with his hands instead of his look. A craving stirred to life inside her, but was it born of lust or a need to temporarily fill the void in her life Liana's passing left and help him in the process? Did she pine for physical distraction from the pain of unmitigated grief, or yearn for what she'd witnessed between the other couple, for what Mitchell had before?

Mitchell slid his hand from her elbow to her hand, tugging her forward with an unreadable expression. "Master Brett, this is our guest tonight, Lillian Gillespie."

"Lillian, my wife and I have heard a little about you." Holding out his hand, Brett checked her face carefully, looking for the bruises that had already disappeared.

"It's nice to meet you. Sir," she tacked on, not wanting to get on anyone's bad side.

He nodded at his wife, who now wore a satin, knee-length robe. "Cindy."

As if she'd been waiting for his permission, Cindy smiled and held out her hand. "So nice to meet you. I hope you're enjoying the club."

"It's an eye-opener," she replied with a rueful grin.

"We need to get going, but I hope you'll come back, Lillian. Mitchell, will we see you at the monthly meeting?"

"I plan on it."

As soon as they were left alone, Lillian rounded on Mitchell with one question before she talked herself out of asking it. "How do I know for sure what I want?"

He scrutinized her face for a moment before replying, "Explore, experiment and find out. I can't answer for you, but I can assist you along the way to discovery, if you're brave enough to take the first step."

She stiffened, narrowing her eyes at the challenge in his tone and behind his words. Between her pulsing body, rioting emotions and that dare, turning him down wasn't an option. Lillian was starting to get a better understanding of what she'd subjected Liana to with her constant challenges.

"How much bossiness do I have to tolerate?"

"I only dish out what is necessary, pet."

Blowing out a breath, Lillian nodded. "What are you suggesting?"

Chapter 9

Lillian would continue to deny it, but the interest in what she'd seen so far was there. Mitchell had watched her pupils darken as he explained the side position on the wheel of misfortune, her nipples harden and face flush as they paused to take in Mindy's writhing body convulsing in climax from a swat that reddened her bare labia and the pulse in her neck jump as they approached Brett and Cindy.

Since returning from dinner at the Dunbars' last night, he had been unable to stop picturing her here, with him tutoring her. Like her, he could admit to lust. What he still couldn't come to terms with was the way she continued to invade his thoughts since meeting her. They shared nothing in common and both agreed they weren't each other's type. Taking a step back as her physician had failed to settle the matter, so that left one more option; to assuage the lust.

"What are you suggesting?"

Her question hung in the air between them. She wouldn't jump into an intense scene, but he could give her a taste of his preferences that might convince her to go a little further. If not, at least they could put whatever this was that kept pulling them together to bed and move on, she to wherever she was headed next and him back to forging a new life without Abbie.

"A better question is what are you willing to try? Light bondage? Public or private, covered, partly bared or naked? The possibilities are endless. Most newbies prefer a secluded spot for their first scene." Her eyes narrowed and fists clenched, signs she didn't like being lumped in with most newbies, as he suspected. The snowball fight she'd initiated at the cabin had given him a glimpse of her competitive streak. In order to take advantage of this opportunity, he would use every bit of knowledge about her to ensure she got the most out of this experience. "Give me something to start with and I'll take it from there."

Lillian's chest lifted as she sucked in a deep breath. "I'm fine with staying up here as long as we're off to the side or in a darker corner. I don't want to be fully restrained, denied all movement." She cast a quick glance behind him at the people in scenes and milling about. "And prefer to start covered." A taunting smile curled her lips as she looked up at him. "Can you do that, *Master* Mitchell."

"A little cautionary advice, pet," he said, clasping her hand, "it's not wise to challenge a Dom." Spotting a vacant spanking bench in the corner, he tugged her over to it. "Wait here a minute while I get a few things."

She tensed next to him, likely from the order, but he didn't look at her as he strode to the cabinet on the wall a few feet away. He didn't have anything in mind until he opened the doors and spotted the thigh straps with attached wrist cuffs. Perfect. Selecting those, he went to the toy cabinet, debating over dildos, vibrators and various spanking implements. A new item caught his eye and he reached for the glass anal beads, his cock twitching as he imagined inserting them, and her response. Picking up the dual slapper and feather tickler, he carried the objects back to Lillian, who eyed them with a mixture of interest and trepidation.

"Remember, saying red ends whatever I'm doing, without

question. If you need to ask me about something, go ahead. Otherwise, try to focus on what your body is saying. Are you wearing panties?"

"Yes, of course."

"Of course," he murmured, watching as she realized his inquiry was appropriate given the different stages of attire by everyone. He unzipped her skirt, keeping his eyes on hers. "You'll still be covered, then, if I remove this. Step out," he instructed as the black garment fell to her feet and left her standing in a pair of beige silk panties and white blouse.

Stooping in front of her, he slid his hands up her smooth right leg. She clutched his shoulders as he reached the top of her thigh and wrapped the Velcro strap. "Drop your right arm."

Her muscles tensed under his hands as she questioned him. "Why?"

Glancing up, he pinned her with a disapproving frown. "Because I said to."

Lillian huffed, those violet eyes swirling with indecision before she gave in to his calm patience and lowered her hand. Mitchell nodded in approval then turned his attention to attaching the cuff to her wrist, binding her arm to her upper thigh, checking to make sure the snug fit wasn't too restricting. He did the same procedure on her left, only he grabbed her hand off his shoulder himself to secure that arm to her leg before pushing to his feet and cupping her chin. "Are you clothed enough and is this dark and secluded enough to continue?"

"Yes." She jerked against the restraints, a confident grin lighting up her face. "I'm not going to freak out on you, Doc."

A part of him wished she would so they could end this and put it behind them. Seeing those long, bare legs again got his blood pumping with a need he couldn't deny, the temptation to test her cocky self-assuredness riding him hard.

"Good to know." Releasing that stubborn jaw, he turned her to face the spanking bench. "Kneel down, hips pressed against the edge, torso prone."

Mitchell had to give her credit for not balking or arguing as she settled into position. Her muscles were tense, her breathing hitched, but she lay facedown on the U-shaped headrest without a word. Testing her, he slid a finger under her panties and grazed the damp seam of her pussy lips. Shifting to the side of the bench while keeping his finger nestled between her puffy labia, he leaned over and whispered in her ear.

"You're wet and swollen, pet. Are you *sure* you're not submissive?"

Lillian lifted and turned her head, their lips almost touching as she replied, "You're touching me, so of course I'm aroused. We've already established that."

"Then let's see if I can confirm a few other things." Straightening, he pressed his finger deeper, brushed against her clit and pulled back. Flicking the side mechanism on the bench, he pushed the head down several inches until her hips were elevated above her shoulders.

Gasping, she yanked on her arms and then groaned at her inability to move. Her voice wobbled, a telltale sign he relished, as she asked, "What are you doing?"

"Placing you in one of my favorite positions." Adding a second finger to her pussy, he stroked her into accepting the decadent pose in favor of concentrating on her pleasure. The next plunge knocked against her womb before he withdrew to circle the small bundle of swollen nerves. Slick juices coated his digits, soft muscles contracted around them and her clit hardened. Time to pull back.

A frustrated growl rumbled from Lillian's throat but, much to his surprise, she kept quiet. Until he coasted his cream-covered fingers up her crack, dampened her anus and then breached the tight puckered entrance with his middle finger up to the first knuckle.

Her whole body quivered as she wheezed, "*Oh, God.* Mitchell, I don't know about *that.*"

"Then say red."

"And stop *everything* now?" she snapped with frustrated incredulity and a shift of her hips.

This was easier than he had hoped. "I guess I can let you skip this experiment, if you can't handle it."

For the first time in what seemed like forever, Mitchell let loose with a deep chuckle as she went rigid and the muffled bite of her reply reached him. "I can handle whatever you want. I'm not saying red, so go ahead."

Working his finger inside her tight ass, he wondered whom he was really testing tonight, himself or her.

"Relax your muscles, concentrate on the sensations."

Relax? Mitchell twisted his finger inside her butt and Lillian wondered how she was supposed to loosen up. She should stop and think before jumping to accept the challenges he kept throwing at her. The inability to move her hands didn't bother her as much as she'd imagined, nor did the mild exhibitionism from losing her skirt. If she were to be honest, both new experiences contributed to her arousal increasing with damp preparedness as he reamed virgin territory with more vigorous strokes.

Fisting her hands for leverage, she took several, lung-filling breaths, exhaling slowly after each one. Her tension eased with every breath and deeper push inside her rectum. He used her own juices to ease his way, the very idea both shocking and stimulating. Thirty-four years old and, as startling ripples of pleasure tingled deep inside that orifice and spread to her pussy, nothing in her past encounters hinted at missing out on anything. With her sheath aching for more attention, she lifted her hips, compressing her lips to contain the verbal plea on the tip of her tongue. One mortification was enough to deal with.

"See? Not so bad, is it?" Mitchell, damn him, pressed his other hand against one buttock and held her hips down. The added restraint increased her vulnerability, inflaming her further, astonishing her with another unpredictable revelation. "You don't need to answer, just continue to concentrate on what your body is telling you."

He pulled slowly out of her clutching inner muscles only to return with two fingers. The minor pinch of pain eased into discomfort as he stretched those muscles with nerve-teasing strokes that caused her vaginal walls to spasm with empty privation. Her panties dampened with the thick cream dripping from her pussy as goosebumps broke out along her perspiration-damp skin. Her nipples ached, pressing against the bench, and the longing to free them of the confines of her clothing intensified with his slow exploration and tantalization of nerve endings she had never considered before.

Without raising her head, she felt him bend to her ear again, his breath warm as he whispered above the low voices, high-pitched cries and other sounds of play going on behind them. "What do you say, Lillian, are you ready for more, or do I stop," he withdrew and then thrust deep in one smooth return plunge, "now, with this?"

Desire for the sweet oblivion of release took over and she shook her head, not needing to think it through. "Don't stop."

Nipping at the tender skin of her neck, he followed the quick sting with warm approval. "You please me, pet."

Lillian tabled the pleasure his praise gave her to delve into later as Mitchell moved back, lifted his hold on her cheek and pulled out of her body and panties. Cooler air wafted over her exposed buttocks as he lowered her panties, the uplifted position of her hips putting her now exposed backside on display. It helped to feel Mitchell's jean-clad legs brushing against her widened inner thighs, knowing his tall, larger frame blocked everyone's direct vision of her. Instead of heated embarrassment, a molten rush of flaming lust sizzled through her veins, aided by the thrust of three fingers filling and stretching her quivering, soaking pussy.

She whimpered, a pathetic sound of need only this man

could pull from her. He played with her clit, pressed against the swollen tissues lining her convulsing sheath and pummeled her depths, but never let those contractions gain momentum toward climax. Her frustration built along with her desperate arousal, her need escaping in a throaty, aching growl.

"Not yet," he stated in a calm, seemingly unaffected tone as her tight grip around his fingers failed to keep them inside her as he pulled back.

"Damn it." She whipped her head up, turning to see him oiling a short strand of different sized glass beads. Suspicion gripped her abdomen as heat flared hotter, both inside and out. "What are those?"

"Anal beads." Mitchell looked at her, running his slick fingers down the shiny orbs. "Do you trust me or want to stop?"

Why did he always have to phrase things in a way that was equivalent to waving a red flag in front of her? His matter-of-fact voice and demeanor prompted her to prove she was no coward as well as attempt to shake that iron control as much and as thoroughly as he had stripped her of her preconceived notions.

"I'll say red when I want to stop," she said, putting her head back down without admitting she trusted him. She wouldn't give an inch where she didn't have to.

Long fingers and a calloused palm gripped one fleshy cheek and squeezed, followed by his gruff baritone. "See that you do."

Lillian gritted her teeth, both against that smug rejoinder and the slow insertion of the smooth glass bulbs. The oil and his hand must have taken the chill off the balls, which helped her accept the foreign objects as they rolled with ease past her tight rim. The first, biggest one was the most difficult to remain still for as it pinched and stretched to the point of soreness. Each consecutive orb was a little smaller and slid easier into place until all five were embedded. The stuffed feeling was unpleasant until she swayed her hips to alleviate the pressure and discovered they rolled and pulsated against those newly exposed nerve endings.

Her astonished cry rent the air before she gasped, "You didn't tell me they *moved*!"

"Vibrate, and it's more fun to show than tell."

Mitchell shifted between her legs, the rough denim against her skin changing to the softer brush of his cotton t-shirt. Those large hands cupped the underside of her buttocks, his thumbs spreading her labia and then the scratch of his goatee tickled her inner thighs as he licked up her seam. Another cry spilled out of her mouth, this one softer as her pussy convulsed around his invading tongue probe.

"Mitchell," she breathed, unsure what she wanted to convey back to him as he lapped at her clit. He didn't stop feasting to answer, thank goodness, adding one long finger to stroke deeper than his tongue could reach.

Between the glass bead's palpitations and his busy tongue and lips, she succumbed to the heightened sensations igniting a heated frenzy throughout her body. A sharp, teeth-tugging yank on her clit elicited a shriek and gush of cream, numbing her to everything except the pleasure spiraling out of control. He lapped over the tortured bud, his finger sliding through her damp channel with ease as he pressed against her slick walls. Sinking his teeth into one tender fold resulted in another convulsive grip around his finger and returning tongue jab.

Lillian forgot about the public exposure, her dislike of Mitchell's bossiness and the fact the activities in this place weren't her thing. As the anal toy and his mouth worked their magic, driving her to the pinnacle of release over and over only to have him slow down enough to stop the final push into orgasm, the reason for her being here, with him in the first place took a back seat to the desperate need he'd kindled inside her. She quaked as every cell was awakened by the painful intensity burning through her system, making her legs shake as she pushed against his marauding mouth in one last, silent plea for an end to his torment.

Instead of showing her mercy, he abandoned her drenched

pussy to tug on the string dangling from her butt. Her muscles tightened around the rolling caress of all five balls but it was the brush of soft feathers teasing her labia that drew a shuddering sigh of pleasure. Swallowing her pride, she opened her mouth to beg but the abrupt snap of leather replacing the feathery caresses seared her tender flesh, drawing a startled shriek instead. She shook as the sting morphed into pulsating heat with another soothing stroke of the feather. "Oh, crap," she groaned as he delivered another burning swat and calming feathery stroke that sent her into a tailspin of needy lust, leaving her no choice but to plead for mercy.

She lifted her head but didn't look back as she pled, "Mitchell, Master, Sir, whatever you want me to call you, *please* do something."

"Tell me what you want," he insisted.

Now she did glance around, grateful he had stood and leaned to the side so she could see him. "Are you really going to make me say it?" she demanded.

"Yes," he returned, the implacable hardness lacing his voice drawing a shiver down her spine. "I can't risk misreading you," he added by way of explanation.

With her hands cuffed at her sides, it was difficult to keep her head raised. Huffing, she swallowed her pride. "Fine, fuck me, is that clear enough for you?"

Mitchell's answer was a blistering smack to both cheeks as he fished a condom out of his pocket. "A little reminder to watch your tone as a matter of respect," he taunted back.

Lillian wanted to smirk in return and tell him the burn only fueled the fire he'd left simmering, but wouldn't put it past him to deny her release. Instead, she opted for a throaty plea. "Please."

"Better." Twirling one finger, he signaled for her to turn around, the silent order grating, but not enough to risk delaying his possession.

As he gripped her hips and prodded her pussy lips with his wide cock head, a sharp barked order from another Dom nearby followed by a leather-snapping lash and shrill cry reminded her of where they were. *What am I doing?* She never imagined she would find herself in such a position, let alone in public. And then Mitchell slid forward, filling her needy pussy with his hard flesh, stretching her sheath with his thickness, and nothing else mattered.

"Take a deep breath, pet."

He didn't give Lillian time to ask why, or to bristle at the disliked endearment as he pulled back with excruciating slowness and tugged on the dangling anal beads cord hard enough to yank the first ball out of her butt. Pleasurable ripples raced up and down both orifices, changing into gripping spasms as he thrust hard and deep with another glass orb release. Like setting flame to a dry timber, she exploded in a burst of fiery contractions, going mindless as he rocked her body on the padded bench with pounding, jackhammer strokes. Sensation after sensation ripped through her with endless pulses, her strangled cries catching on breathless sobs.

Mitchell didn't know what got to him more, Lillian's acceptance of everything he'd introduced her to thus far or the tight contractions of her slick heat squeezing his cock. Yes, he thought with licks of pleasure traversing up and down his pummeling shaft, it had been weeks since he'd indulged in fucking a sub, but he'd abstained for a full year following Abbie's death and hadn't experienced this intense conflagration of gripping satisfaction when he'd first returned to their Denver club.

Tabling those thoughts in favor of enjoying the snug, welcoming pussy pulling his climax up from his balls, he released the last anal bead, relishing the unconscious lift of her ass and shuddering, sweat-dampened body. Leaning over, he braced his hands on the bench at her sides, grunting as he proceeded to ride her hard and fast with rapid hip-jerking thrusts.

Lillian's second climax spasmed around his pistoning shaft, the final, irresistible lure to letting go with his own orgasm. His head filled with the euphoria of pleasure spewing up his cock and bursting into the latex cover. The bench shook from the force of his ramming hips but she continued to embrace his rough possession with toe-pushing ass-lifting that provided a soft cushion for him to land on.

It took several seconds to clear his head and get his breath back as he soaked up the tiny quivers of her swollen, wet muscles still teasing his flesh. Attuned to her every sound and movement, he heard the moment her heavy breathing and satisfied moans hitched into a tortured sob, and then another and another.

Lifting off her, Mitchell released her wrists with one hand while removing the condom with the other. Coming around the bench, he discarded the protection in a bin and reached for her shaking shoulders, guessing the dam burst on her pent-up emotions before she could rouse from the euphoria enough to put her shields back up.

"I've got you, Lillian." Her weeping continued as she stood and allowed him to pull up her panties without a word. She didn't snipe or complain when he lifted her, just buried her face in his shoulder and shook with the strength of her torrential outburst as he carried her downstairs and into the secluded nook, away from curious, concerned eyes.

This breakdown, he suspected as he settled on the small sofa behind plant-topped half-walls, centered more on grief than what her first lifestyle scene revealed about her sexual makeup. She was a strong woman and would either embrace that new knowledge about herself or walk away from exploring it further. But he knew only too well there was no way to dismiss the agonizing heartbreak of loss that cut so deep it left you numb for months. Her grief was still in its infancy compared to his, which meant she was still coming to terms with her sister's death, with the fact she would never see or speak with her again, that their special bond was forever severed.

His heart ached as she burrowed deeper with a wrenching, watery hiccup and he recalled the devastation and pain of losing Abbie. Tightening his arms around her shivering body, he leaned his head back and let her cry it out, wishing there was something, anything he could say or do to ease her pain.

Devin entered the quiet corner holding out Lillian's black skirt with a worried look in his dark blue eyes. "Is she all right?"

"She will be, she just doesn't know it yet." His friend must have seen Mitchell's own sorrow reflected on his face because he nodded and laid the garment on the arm of the sofa.

"Greg and I will be at the bar with Kelsey. If you need her, or Nan, text one of us."

Damn, it was good to allow himself the benefits of friendships again. "Thanks. Appreciate it." As soon as Devin left, Lillian tensed and pulled away.

Dropping his arms, he let her get to her feet and reach for her skirt. She pulled it on in silence, keeping her splotched, tear-streaked face averted. He could empathize with her need to be alone, to work on assimilating through what prompted her loss of control. Once she did that, the questions about her compliance upstairs would start.

"I need to find Nan, see if she's ready to leave," Lillian said, her voice scratchy as she turned to face him with a closed expression.

Understanding made him more inclined to give her space, but not to turn over her welfare to someone else. Pushing to his feet, he grabbed her hand. "I'll take you. Returning to Willow Springs is out of Nan's way and it's ridiculous since we're going to the same location."

"You're ready to go? Isn't it early for you?"

"No."

They stopped at the bar, where Dan was now serving, to let him and Nan know they were leaving. The satisfied glow in Nan's eyes and rosy complexion were telltale signs of Dan's expertise in seeing to his wife's needs. The smile hovering on her lips reminded Mitchell how much he used to enjoy assuaging Abbie's cravings. With a jolt, he realized he had derived as much contentment from introducing Lillian to the club scene and public play as he'd had pleasuring his spouse. It was time, he decided, to do some soul-searching and figure out what it was about Lillian that stoked feelings he thought he'd buried with Abbie.

"I'm taking Lillian home," he addressed Nan before looking at her husband. "Do you mind making my excuses for skipping out on monitor duty tonight?"

One glance at Lillian's ravaged face was all Dan needed to give his support. "No problem, we have plenty of help even without Caden and Connor. Lillian, I hope we see you again."

Nan reached over and squeezed her hand. "I'll call you," was all she said, but it was enough for Lillian to nod in appreciation.

"Okay, thanks. Goodnight."

As Mitchell walked her out and she continued to ignore him, he was honest enough with himself to admit to the dent she'd put in his ego almost from their first encounter. He'd had women come on to him over the years, as both a Dom and a doctor, a few disregarding his marital status until he set them straight. Lillian had made her disinterest in him clear from the onset. He enjoyed tonight more than he thought he would, her telling expressions, bravado in going through with a scene and the tight clasp of her wet pussy pleasing him in different ways. Her meltdown affected him on a different level, one that tugged at those emotions he thought had died three years ago.

Because he found himself working through his own affecting upheaval, he allowed her to stay silent until he parked in front of his garage. Turning in the seat, he stated quietly, "Grief isn't something you can rush or put a time limit on. I can tell you it will lessen and getting through the days will get easier, but not when. How did your sister die?"

He wasn't sure she would answer, but she took a shuddering breath, let it out on a sigh and said, "A brain aneurysm, followed by six weeks in a coma. I know she never would have recovered, or if she'd come out of it, she would have had severe brain damage and I'm not sure that would have been any easier to live with."

Mitchell winced. What she described was truly a worst-case scenario for any family member to have to cope with. "I'm sorry. My wife suffered through cancer treatments before she passed away and it took me a long time to see past my grief enough to admit relief that she was free of that agony. Come on. I'll walk you up. Go to bed, you need the sleep."

He came around the SUV, not surprised she hadn't waited for him to open the door. Sidestepping his reach for her hand, she started for the stairs, her back as rigid as her tone. "You're ordering me around again, and I don't need you to walk me up."

"Too bad." Moving ahead of her, he climbed the stairs and held out his hand for the key. She slapped it into his palm with an exasperated huff that made his lips twitch. "Good girl," he praised her and got the rise he'd expected.

"I'm not a girl and don't need your praise."

"It's my job to know what you need." Opening the door, he flicked on the overhead light and handed her back the key. "I aced anatomy, pet, and seen you naked. Trust me, you're a girl. What?" he asked sharply, her nose crinkling as she sniffed and frowned.

"Smells funny in here, smokey."

He caught a faint pungent odor, not enough to pinpoint a source or name it. "Could be the furnace. It's old. I'll have someone out to check it this week." Cupping her chin, he refused to let her jerk out of his hold, enjoying the flash in those amethyst eyes as he examined her face, ensuring she would be okay once he left. The temptation to lean down and kiss that mulish mouth was another indication his feelings for her were reaching a level he never thought to experience again. He hadn't kissed a woman since Abbie. "Call me tonight if you have trouble getting to sleep." Brushing his thumb across the plump softness of her lower lip, he rumbled, "Goodnight, Lillian."

Lillian locked the door behind Mitchell and leaned against it, still working on coming to grips with her shattered physical and emotional control. She had caved to his sexual dominance as fast as she'd crumbled into an uncontrollable sobbing heap afterward. From what she witnessed, he'd gone easy on her, likely due to her inexperience and denial. But there was more than the destruction of her preconceived notions about herself she was having trouble reconciling with. The welcoming comfort of his arms wrapped around her, his caring, protective hold and considerate silence while she fell apart had barely registered until he released her to feel bereft and alone.

Pushing away from the door, Lillian bemoaned the lingering ache for Mitchell's solicitous attention that was *so* unlike her. Her body still vibrated with pleasure she'd reaped from taking his orders and his cock, her mind numb from the unexpected meltdown and continuing need for his comfort. She needed to get a handle on this undesirable complication with a man who defined everything she disliked about the opposite sex.

She was too drained to reason it all out tonight, so she padded to the computer to check her email before going to bed. Her agent was working on several promotions for her and the sooner she heard back from him, the quicker she could plan where to go from here. Her nose twitched from the faint odor that was strong enough on this side of the room to make her eyes water the same as she suffered during allergy season. The low hum of the furnace gave credence to Mitchell's explanation until she sat down at the corner desk and the screen popped up as if she hadn't shut it down before leaving. A coil of suspicion cramped her abdomen as she inspected the desk and floor for signs someone had been in here.

Not seeing anything, she relaxed and blamed exhaustion for her paranoid thoughts, went through her emails without finding anything from her agent and shut down the computer and her wayward emotions for the night.

Chapter 10

Bryan returned to his motel room, the drink he stopped for after leaving Lillian's apartment empty handed doing little to ease his frustration. Dropping onto the bed, he locked his hands behind his head and stared up at the ceiling, wishing it weren't too late to call the hospital and check on Brad. The hour he risked searching her computer and then the apartment had yielded nothing. His brother never had made protecting him easy. The lectures during Brad's rebellious teen years had fallen on deaf ears and he'd despaired of his younger sibling ever putting his high IQ to good use. And then Brad had surprised him by acing four years of college in three and getting accepted into medical school. There had been a few bumps along the way, such as DUIs and two ex-girlfriends who filed assault charges after he'd broken off the relationship.

As if, he snorted. No one, least of all him believed their unsubstantiated, wild accusations. Brad was never without a line of women waiting to jump at the chance to enter into an affair with one of the city's most successful, wealthiest doctors and the few who were awarded the privilege each thought she would be the one he would keep. He could see Brad getting frustrated with a woman who refused to walk away without causing a scene when he was done with her, but a few bruises didn't add up to assault.

But attacking his brother with enough surprise and force to leave him with a debilitating head wound was battery, and unforgivable in his book. No way would he return home without destroying those pictures first. He refused to let her drag Brad's good name and reputation through the mud because she couldn't accept he was done with her. She needed to pay for her sins. He would have to get hold of her phone somehow, as that was the next logical device where he would find anything. Assuming she carried it with her, he needed to take care plotting his next step. Breaking in again would be the easy part considering the quick way he'd manipulated the flimsy lock tonight without leaving a trace. Entering the residence while she was sleeping increased the risk to him and his career, but what other choice did she leave him?

Unfortunately, time was not on his side. Between the two-day drive here and the days of tracking her whereabouts, he didn't have the luxury of waiting. If Bryan could get in tomorrow night, grab her phone and get out quick, Lillian would never suspect or hear a thing. With luck, she'd think she lost her cell, he could dispose of it and the photos and return to Utah to assist Brad in filing a complaint he would ensure resulted in charges.

As long as everything went according to plan.

Mitchell spent Sunday resisting the urge to check on Lillian, reminding himself she was fine when he left her last night. That determined independence continued to annoy him when he was in Dom mode as much as he admired the strength it took to make her way alone in the world. After the numerous cases of abuse he'd seen come through the emergency room over the years, he had gotten a good idea of how difficult it was for women to walk away from such toxic relationships. He still didn't know much about Lillian's circumstances, and that was on him. He hadn't pushed, figuring first, they wouldn't see each other again after she left the cabin and second, when they did, their opposing personalities and desires would prevent any type of relationship from forming.

It was hard to admit he was wrong, and this morning, even more difficult to acknowledge he hadn't a clue where to go from here. The temptation to kiss her and reluctance to walk away last night were additional signs he should take the time for soul-searching before going forward. Was he ready and willing to explore taking their odd pairing further than any other relationship since losing Abbie? And if so, how to get Lillian on board with the idea remained an obstacle.

To take his mind off the promise of her acceptance of what she'd not only witnessed last night but everything he'd put her through, he trudged up to the attic to go through Abbie's things, a chore he'd put off for too long. Opening the door to the musty odor, he flicked on the light, his eyes landing on her wedding dress hanging in the corner. Padding over to it, he fingered the lacey cream satin, picturing her shy smile as she'd walked toward him down the aisle. The memories could still produce a small pang and there would always be a small corner of his heart just for her and the special bond they had shared as both husband and wife and Dom/sub.

Would he really accept anything less in another relationship? Lillian's flashing eyes and taunting smirks replaced Abbie's downcast subservience and soft smiles of pleasure at doing his bidding. Lillian would challenge him, and maybe, since he had traded the everyday stress of sixty-hour workweeks as the head ER physician and trauma surgeon at a large hospital for the less time-consuming, mentally straining job of family practitioner, he would find the change stimulating. But would Lillian?

Mitchell took the dress off the rack and folded it up. Grabbing an empty box, he started gathering other items he had stashed up here when he moved in, at the time, still unable to let go of anything. With luck, bringing closure to one part of his life would help decide which path to take toward a possible new beginning.

Lillian took off early Sunday morning, enjoyed a big breakfast at the diner and visiting with people she was still getting to know. By the time she left, the sun shone high in the sky, the temperature already hitting the fifty-degree mark. She drove to the city park, acres of trees surrounding a small lake she discovered a few days ago. The picnic tables were empty but a few kids played on the playground and several people were taking advantage of the nice day to follow the walking path that wound in and out of the woods. Paddleboats sat docked but she could picture them in use during the summer months. After taking several pictures, she sat at a table with her sketch pad, sighing as she opened it to the picture of Liana she'd drawn at Mitchell's cabin.

As always, sorrow threatened to bring her down, just like this morning when she'd first awoken and wanted to talk to Liana about her tumultuous feelings over surrendering to Mitchell and his sexual preferences. It wasn't the first time and, God help her, she hoped it wouldn't be the last. She could call Nan or Avery to talk out her confusion, but as welcoming and encouraging as her new friends were, they lacked the years of knowing her better than anyone else and the insight her special bond with her twin had offered.

"What do you say, sis? Is it time to pack up and go? Out of sight, out of mind, that's all I need to get over this weird infatuation, right?" The picture didn't answer, her mumblings drawing curious looks from a couple walking by and an immediate, painful twinge. The longer she stayed in Willow Springs, the more she wanted to stick around. Flipping the page over, she eyed the sketch of Mitchell and her heart turned over, proof she didn't need her sister to tell her she didn't want to go. Not yet.

She spent another hour at the park drawing and then returned to the apartment to paint. Nan called, asking how she was handling her first BDSM scene, her concern reminding Lillian of everyone's unconditional acceptance of her into their close-knit group of friends. "Like you've been telling me, Doctor Mitchell is a hard man to resist," she'd admitted. She didn't mention embracing the physical responses to his sexual control was easy compared to the dent her acceptance put in her sworn independent nature. She couldn't have it both ways – a sexually submissive desire while keeping her liberated views – could she? Wasn't that at the root of her constant indecision since meeting Mitchell?

Between the time Lillian fixed dinner and turned in for the night, the answer to that question still evaded her. But as she drifted to sleep, there was no doubt how much time she spent that day craving to see Mitchell and hear his deep voice issuing more of those sexual demands she couldn't resist.

Bryan waited another fifteen minutes after the lights went out in both the house and garage apartment before making a stealthy return back up the side steps and crouching to work the flimsy lock again. Clamping his cigarette between his lips, he slid the credit card between the door and lock, grateful the people in this backwoods town were dumb enough to leave themselves vulnerable to such break-ins. At least something was going his way.

A hall night light shed just enough illumination for him to make out the lowered Murphy bed and Lillian's sleeping form, something he hadn't counted on. His smoke might awaken her, but if he put it out, the ashes would leave evidence of his presence. Moving fast while keeping quiet wasn't easy but he refused to back out now. He found her purse sitting next to the painting easel propped in front of the window. Keeping low, he searched the bag, gripped the phone and sidled back out the door, never noticing the ashes that dropped onto the turpentine-soaked rag next to the paints.

A faint, familiar odor tickled Lillian's nose and throat several groggy minutes before the crackle of fire and wisps of smoke awoke her other senses. Coughing, she blinked open watery eyes to see flames licking up the window curtains and spreading to the ceiling. Shocked terror galvanized her into action as she threw herself from the bed and stumbled toward the door. She was halfway there when Mitchell flung it open, bare-chested and barefoot, gripping a fire extinguisher in one hand as he yanked her out with the other.

"Get downstairs," he barked before entering the room with the fire-dousing spray already spewing from the canister.

Lillian dashed down the stairs and was greeted with the wail of sirens disturbing the quiet residential street. Wearing nothing but a thigh length sleep shirt and panties, she stood to the side, shivering as a volunteer fire truck pulled to the curb and a sheriff's cruiser behind it. One of the young firemen tossed her a blanket as the deputy approached her with his hand out.

"Ma'am. Why don't you sit in my vehicle while we get this under control and then you can give me a statement."

Too shook up and cold to say anything, she nodded and slid into the still running SUV, savoring the heat as she watched with dread. An hour passed in which firemen dragged a hose up the stairs and aimed another hose spray at the side of the garage, working to contain the blaze still sparking inside the apartment. At one point, one of them had carried out several of her paintings and stacked them on the front porch of the house before trotting back up. Sheriff Grayson arrived thirty minutes ago and joined Mitchell upstairs, her worry for everyone increasing the longer it took to get the fire under control.

With a sigh of relief, Lillian finally saw the firemen rolling up their hoses and tromping down the stairs from the blackened garage. Mitchell's soot darkened face looked as grim as Grayson's as they came toward the cruiser. Opening the door, Mitchell took her hand, tugging her out as she noticed the plastic sack clutched in his other hand.

"Come inside, pet. We need to talk."

That, along with the questions and concern crossing both men's faces caused Lillian's throat to clog with anxiety. Holding the blanket closed with her other hand, worry kept her silent until Mitchell opened the front door. "What's wrong?" she asked as soon as she entered his house for the first time.

"Sit down." He led her into a living room and pointed to a leather sectional in front of a brick fireplace. Setting the bag on the floor, he said, "I managed to grab your purse, some clothing and the bank bag that was stashed under it. Everything left reeks too much of smoke to salvage."

"Thanks." Flicking a glance toward the sheriff, whose rigid, arms-crossed stance made her nervous, she asked, "What happened? Was it the furnace?" The look they exchanged didn't promise an easy explanation and spiked up her anxiety another notch. Mitchell leaned against the fireplace, his biceps bulging as he too crossed his arms. Before tonight, the only time she'd seen him bare chested had been at the cabin, when she eyed his complete nakedness as he turned from the fire and lust had tempered her grief for a short span. But right now, with her nerves shot, his overbearing, overprotective stance and intent gaze was working for her.

"The fire started by your paint supplies, the rags next to your easel," Grayson said. "Turpentine is highly flammable."

Lillian jumped to her feet, her body taut with denial. "Those are kept in a metal bucket and never near a furnace, or even a vent. And I don't smoke. You have to be wrong." Because if he wasn't, that meant she was responsible for the destruction of Mitchell's property, and she couldn't bear that.

"Lillian, you're not to blame." Mitchell's sharp rebuttal drew her stricken gaze. "Before turning in, did you lock the door?"

"Yes. I always do."

"Exactly. Like me, coming from a big city, we automatically lock our homes, coming and going. Your door was not only unlocked when I arrived, but not even latched. We," he nodded toward Grayson, "believe someone entered after you fell asleep."

Remembering the indistinct odor she had caught the last two evenings upon entering the apartment and finding her computer on after she shut it down before leaving, she sank back down on the sofa wondering what they had been after. Shaking her head, she glanced from Mitchell to Grayson, confused. "I don't have anything worth taking, except maybe the laptop, which was still there."

"Why don't you tell us about your ex, his name for starters?" Grayson insisted, a hard glint in his eyes.

"Brad?" Unable to help it, she scoffed at the idea. "Trust me, if he even bothered to go to the trouble of tracking down my whereabouts, he would confront me face to face. He was all about control." She sent Mitchell a rueful grin. "A lot like you, but in a destructive way. Funny, he's a well-established surgeon, his brother's a cop." Her eyes slid back to Grayson. "And now I find myself answering to another physician and cop. I gotta tell you, I don't like it."

"Too bad, and don't compare us to them. We both saw the evidence of your ex's destructive control," Mitchell reminded her, not at all amused by her comparison.

"What's his last name and I'll judge whether he is worth checking up on. How long were you together and what was the catalyst that made you leave?" Grayson returned with cool insistence.

Lillian recoiled from saying anything else about her relationship with Brad. She averted her face from Grayson's probing stare and Mitchell's unwavering gaze, afraid they would see the shame she couldn't shake since she didn't regret willingly sharing Brad's bed after he would hit her. She couldn't bear to have them judge her, not any of these people who had welcomed her into their intimate group and friendly community. Brad's threats to cause Liana pain if Lillian didn't go along brought her more angst than letting him rut on top of her for ten minutes a few times. The sex with him before she broke off their initial relationship had been good, making it easier to tolerate his touch again without enjoying it.

"McCabe, and I'm not discussing our relationship. It wasn't Brad, that's all I'll say." She shivered again, unable to dispel the chills still racking her body. It was hard to wrap her head around finding herself a victim of a crime here in this peaceful, small town after avoiding that fate living her entire life in the big city. "It must have been kids or a random attempt at theft, not realizing someone was occupying the space."

Grayson cut his gray/green gaze to Mitchell, his shadowed jaw taut. "I'll wait for the fire inspector's report later this week." His hard tone signaled he would return at that time to continue questioning her.

Pushing to her feet again, guilt over his damaged property prompted her to apologize even though she wasn't at fault, and there was no way Brad was involved. "I'm sorry, Mitchell. I'll pay…"

"Fuck that, Lillian," Mitchell snapped out with an angry slice of his hand as he gave in to the urge to go to her. He never imagined anything could scare him as much as reading Abbie's test results confirming stage four cancer until he'd seen smoke obscuring the window of the garage apartment. As he tore out of his house with his abdomen knotted into a painful twist of fear, one thought kept repeating itself; he couldn't lose another woman he cared about. Now, after admitting and accepting that revelation, seeing Lillian turn away from their astute gazes, looking ashamed and refusing to answer their probing questions about her asshole ex, then hearing her apologize and offer to pay for some intruder's careless destruction prompted him to act.

Surprise erased the guilt on her face as he gripped her arms and hauled her up against him. Instead of changing in a flash to irritation, which was her usual reaction when he pressed the control issue, her eyes went dark with arousal, an ache tightening her face as she leaned into him. Neither paid attention as Grayson walked out.

"Whatever is going on is not your fault. We will get to the bottom of it, but until then, it's time for both of us to quit dancing around what's going on between us." Without giving her a chance to answer, he swooped down and covered those soft lips with his mouth, kissing a woman for the first time since Abbie. And damned if it didn't feel right, regardless she was all wrong for him and he for her.

The blanket dropped to their feet as her low moan echoed from her mouth into his when she opened for him. Her breasts flattened against his chest, the rigid nipples a sharp contrast to the plump softness cushioning his tense muscles. Exploring her mouth with tongue-stroking thoroughness, he slid his hands down and under the nightshirt to palm her buttocks, grinding his cock against her mound. Demanding need born of fear and frustration overrode any lingering doubts about going down this path with a woman he had thought unsuitable for his desires. As her arms squeezed his shoulders and one long, smooth leg wrapped around his thigh, it was obvious her current needy state burned as hot and fast as his. For now, that was enough.

Letting go of her right cheek, Mitchell gripped a fist full of Lillian's deep red hair and tugged her head back as he released her mouth from the hard pressure of his possession. "Now," he demanded. Spinning her around, he pushed against her shoulders, urging her to bend down to the couch. "Brace your hands on the seat."

"Mitchell." She groaned his name, swaying her hips as he shoved the silken top up and yanked down the black panties to bare her lily-white ass.

A hard swat left behind a bright red imprint and drew a

shudder, but she didn't move from the position. "That's Sir, or Master Mitchell when I have you naked."

She whipped her head around and gave him a narrow-eyed glare. "You're doing it again."

He cupped her damp pussy. "Want me to stop?"

"No way." She huffed and turned back around, muttering, "Sir."

Another smack reddened her opposite buttock. "That's what I thought." Fingering her wet pussy, he released his cock and sheathed himself, the urgency to take and possess riding him hard. Slick, swollen muscles clamped around his pumping finger, the rucked-up top giving him an enticing view of her dangling, hard-tipped breasts. Nudging her feet further apart with his foot, he stepped between her spread legs and replaced his finger with his shaft, sliding smoothly between her plump labia.

"*Yes.*"

Lillian's breathy acceptance coincided with the tight clutch of wet vaginal walls around his cock, drawing him deeper inside her. Mitchell leaned over her back, reached around and filled his hands with her breasts as he said into her ear, "Fast and hard, pet. Brace yourself."

As promised, or threatened, depending on how she took that warning, he tweaked her nipples, straightened and held her hips still for a deep, carnal fucking. Her grunts and heavy breathing matched his as he rammed into her quivering depths over and over, the spasming clutches of her pussy pulling his climax forward too soon but with irresistible force.

"Shit, Lillian," he ground out as she splintered in orgasm around him with a cry and tight squeezes. She didn't say anything, just shook her head as her elbows gave out and she lay facedown on her bent arms emitting softer mewls.

Mitchell saw stars as he exploded into the latex with faster, harder strokes, as if he couldn't get enough. He hadn't come that hard in years, and as Abbie's image filled his head, he prayed she approved because there was no going back for him. Now, as his head cleared and he pulled out of her still gripping body, he had to figure out how to get Lillian on board.

"You'll stay in my room, with me, while you're here."

Okay, I can do this, Lillian decided as Mitchell tossed her over his shoulder and carried her toward the back of the house. Calling him Sir hadn't been difficult, not with her lust skyrocketing with that purposeful look on his face as he'd hauled her against his wide, warm chest, ridding her of the body-numbing cold. As soon as she'd come into contact with his body heat and his mouth, it had been so easy to give in to his control, let him take her over and not have to think, just feel.

She laughed as he tossed her on his bed and whisked her night shirt over her head. "This he-man stuff doesn't work for me," she insisted, her heartbeat going haywire as he ripped her panties off.

"Prove it." Mitchell spread her legs, his eyes traveling from her gaping pussy to her face, nailing her with one of those fixed gazes that said he was focused solely on her and no one or nothing else.

Her humor fled as he trailed a finger up her slit then down her crack to dampen that taboo orifice, drawing her attention to the pinprick tingles from those slaps still racing across her buttocks as she shifted on the bed. She still struggled with understanding how one man could cause her pain she wanted nothing to do with and another make her burn and ache for the blistering sting of his hand connecting with her bare flesh.

"You're thinking too hard." Mitchell kept his eyes on hers as he continued to glide up and down between pussy and anus while stroking his semi-erection into a steel rod.

His salt and pepper hair hung in disheveled thickness around his face and neck, soot still stained his cheek and chest and those firm lips were set in a tight line as he waited for acceptance. Arousal replaced conflicting thoughts and she arched into his hand. "You're right." Reaching up, she gripped his forearms and pleaded, "Fuck me again, *please.*"

"Please what?" he asked in a silky steel voice as he dragged his cock up between her cheeks and through her slick pussy lips.

Lillian gave in with a shudder. "Sir." He filled her with a single, womb-bouncing plunge, wrenching a cry from her constricted throat and abolishing all thoughts except one. *More.*

Bryan couldn't believe it. Letting himself into his motel room, he grabbed the bottle of bourbon on the desk and poured himself a hefty swallow. He still shook inside, unable to comprehend how he could have been so careless. With disgust, he stubbed out the cigarette. He'd barely made it back to his car around the corner from the doctor's residence when the wail of sirens came screeching up the street. When the fire truck and cops pulled in front of the garage he'd just broken into, he noticed the smoke drifting out of the open upstairs door as Lillian came running down the stairs. Nervous sweat still ran down his back to pool at the base of his spine.

Lifting the bottle, he skipped the glass and took the next long pull from the container as his wobbly legs gave out and he sank down onto the bed. B and E was one thing, and in this case, the ends justified the means. But causing a fire that could have taken a life was something he never would have attempted intentionally, not even for his brother. He fished her cell phone out of his back pocket, swearing when he couldn't find any pictures. *Jesus, all for nothing again.* Tossing the phone on the bed, he reached for his and pressed Brad's hospital number, hoping he was awake, and if so, he would have his cell.

"Where the hell are you?" Brad's tired voice came through the line and relief eased Bryan's tension.

"In Billings, Montana, and it's nice to hear from you, too. You gave me quite a scare, little brother."

"Sorry. I guess I'm not infallible after all. Why the hell are you in Montana?" he grumbled.

"Because this is where I tracked your assaulting ex to. I managed to search her computer and now have her phone, but can't find any pictures of herself with bruises. I think she lied to you." Exasperation colored his tone as he took another swig of alcohol, his earlier blunder still haunting him.

There was a long pause and some cursing before Brad snapped, "I told you to let it go. Why didn't you listen?"

"Because I'm not letting her get away with landing you where you're at now. Fuck that, Brad, you could have died from her jealous assault." And that still scared him, even more than coming close to causing real physical harm to Lillian tonight.

"She takes pictures with a high-resolution camera that she usually keeps in her car, but, seriously, Bryan, leave her be. I'll recover and be back on my feet in no time."

Brad's tired voice reminded him how close he'd come to dying, and made it difficult to nix his plan to bring Lillian in. "Get some rest. I'll head back and be there before you're discharged," he replied, but not before he got that camera. He couldn't risk her or the cops connecting him to the fire tonight, leaving him no choice but to set aside his desire for justice, like Brad wanted. But the least Bryan could do was ensure she didn't return with her blackmail threat in the future.

Chapter 11

Lillian had slept like a baby spooned in front of Mitchell, her buttocks nestled against his groin, his bearded chin resting on her head with his arm wrapped around her waist. It was a shame she awoke alone, she thought as she slid out of bed. She would have enjoyed going another round with him. From the first moment they'd met, he had known exactly what she needed to get through whatever phase of grief or adjustment she was struggling with and it still baffled her how she could accept and enjoy his sexual dominance when everything in her rebelled at giving a man, any man, an ounce of control over her. Living under the strain of Brad's depraved threats for a month should have soured her for good against all men. She was honest enough with herself to admit something had changed and clicked that last night at Mitchell's cabin when he unselfishly set aside his desire to spend that time alone to deal with his own loss to aid her in coping with Liana's death.

Picking up the bag of belongings he had gathered from the smoke-ruined apartment, she padded into the attached bathroom marveling at how far she'd come in such a short time. And all due to someone she never would have believed could slip past her shield of independence.

Nothing to do about it now except go forward, she mused as she went through the meager remains of clothing left to her. Two pairs of pants, jeans and slacks, one long-sleeved top, a tee shirt and a pullover sweater. The only underwear she now possessed were the ripped panties lying on the bedroom floor. "I'm a perv," she muttered as a heated thrill swept through her that she denied aloud. "He might like to go commando, but not me." First on her agenda today was a shopping trip into Billings. Make that second, she amended when her stomach growled.

Lillian helped herself to a shower and dressed in the jeans and top before opening her purse to see what make-up items she might still have inside. Right off she realized her phone was missing and prayed it had dropped out when Mitchell picked up her bag. She found him in the torn-apart kitchen, his cell to his ear as he flicked her an assessing, head-to-toe look before finishing his call.

"Thanks, Maggie. I'll be in by noon. What's wrong?" he asked as soon as he clicked off.

"You know, I may have come around to your way of thinking when it comes to sex, but I still dislike how you can read me with such accuracy. It's just creepy."

"Deal with it and answer my question."

Okay, this part of his bossiness she did not care for. "Look, Mitchell…"

He stalked toward her but she held her ground, lifting her chin as he stood toe to toe with her. "Someone was upstairs with you, while you were sleeping, vulnerable to whatever crime he wanted to commit. Stow your objections to my officiousness until we figure out who, and why."

Lillian took a deep, calming breath and nodded. Pointing out the danger to her last night of an even worse crime than breaking and entering doused her annoyance with the effectiveness of a splash of cold water to the face. "Fine, for now. My cell is missing. It probably fell out in the apartment. I need to get in and look for it."

He shook his head with a frown. "I picked up your purse by the top and kept it closed, but we'll check. If we don't find it, our first stop is the sheriff's office."

"Don't you have to get to work?" she asked as he steered her out the front door.

"Not for a few hours. The clinic's receptionist is rescheduling my morning appointments. This, and you are more important."

She tried not to read too much into that grumbled statement that gave her a warm fuzzy. They didn't find her phone in the smoke-damaged apartment, or any clothing that didn't reek to the point of rendering it unsalvageable, so they drove to the precinct where Grayson was waiting for them. "What's on your phone that someone would take such a risk for?" Grayson questioned as he wrote down her information.

"There's nothing of importance on it, no banking information or credit cards. I'm very careful about that, so it had to be random."

"No, it didn't." Grayson leaned back in his chair, removed the toothpick from his mouth and dropped a bombshell on her. "You wouldn't happen to have anything to do with Brad McCabe being in the hospital, recovering from a brain bleed caused by a concussion, would you?"

Shock drained the blood from Lillian's face, and it was only Mitchell's large hand closing over hers on the armrest of the chair that kept her grounded as she worked her mind around that startling information. "I had no idea," she murmured. "I swear, he was fine when I left, maybe a little dazed, but good enough to continue his tirade against my leaving." She looked from the sheriff to Mitchell, resigned to reliving that morning for their benefit. "My sister was pronounced brain dead that morning, following six weeks in a coma and…" She paused, refusing to mention Brad's blackmail, the reason she stayed. "And I'd had enough, wanted out to be alone to grieve. You should understand that," she said to Mitchell, her tone accusatory with frustration.

"Continue," was all he said.

Shrugging, she gave them the bare bones. "He came home to find me packed up, ready to go except for two large paintings I was carrying downstairs. I wasn't expecting him, but he'd heard about Liana. He came at me, the first time he ever went for my face, and I realized how far he was willing to go this time. After the kick to my ribs, I managed to get up and swing the one painting I still held at him. The frame caught his temple and he went down. I ran out with him well enough to curse me, able to get help if he needed it. That was weeks ago."

There was no censure or criticism on either man's face. Grayson kept writing as he replied, "Since that's out of my jurisdiction, I can't get a doctor's report. I'm waiting to hear back from his brother, hoping he'll be open to talking."

Lillian scoffed. "Don't count on it. Bryan idolizes his baby brother, covers for him every time Brad gets so much as a speeding ticket." Pushing to her feet, she gave in to the need for fresh air. "I have things to do. Are we done here?"

"For now." Grayson nodded at Mitchell and he clasped her hand again and led her out.

As soon as they stepped out of the small precinct, she rounded on him, insisting, "I'm fine, before you ask. If you'll take me back to get my car, you can get to work."

"After breakfast. So you know," he added, setting out toward the diner, "you will eventually have to reveal the rest of the story between you and McCabe."

Lillian didn't reply. She had enough to think about to keep her on edge for a while.

Mitchell hated that cloud of shame that darkened Lillian's eyes whenever he mentioned her ex. She wasn't a meek woman, or gullible, which meant there was a reason she'd stayed with the bastard after the first abusive incident. He tried not to push her for answers – at first because it was none of his business and he had believed he would never see her again after she left his cabin. Since then, he'd been waging a battle with himself over his growing interest in her and how far he was willing to let it go. He never considered another committed relationship was in the cards for him, and had been content with being among the lucky few who got to spend years with that one special person everyone hoped they would meet.

After taking her back to his place, he drove to the clinic admitting he wanted it all again, this time with someone who was the complete opposite of his beloved Abbie and yet, perfect for him as much as his wife had been. Lillian would keep him on his toes, challenge his dominant side and fill the void Abbie's death had left in his life. He didn't question how he could love two such opposite women, not after learning the hard way how short life really was. He didn't go looking for another relationship, but he wasn't going to waste any more time denying what was staring him in the face after she'd come so close to real harm from that fire.

Mitchell went into his office before seeing the first patient and checked his calendar for the week. The clinic appointments were light, but he started his new once-a-week position as the on-call trauma surgeon at All Saints Hospital in Billings on Friday. As much as he had reaped the benefits of an easier, slower professional pace since relocating here, he had discovered he didn't want to let his surgical skills lapse all together. Seeing no appointments scheduled as of yet on Wednesday afternoon, he blocked those hours off, planning to take Kurt up on his offer to bring Lillian out to the ranch for a ride. Leslie, a grade school teacher, was off this week for spring break, and the more he could aid Lillian in cultivating friendships here, the easier it would be to talk her into staying.

Between now and then, he was sure he could come up with a scene to take her mind off her troubles and demonstrate, once again, how much she enjoyed his sexual kinks.

For the first time since losing Abbie, Mitchell returned home after work without dreading the emptiness waiting for him. With signs of spring popping up came longer days and he found Lillian on the back porch perched in front of her easel wearing a paint-splattered smock and sad expression. She looked up as he stepped outside and those expressive eyes masked whatever she had been thinking about as a small smile tilted the corners of her lips.

"What's up, Doc?"

"My hunger." It was his turn to grin when arousal swirled in her eyes. "For dinner first, pet." She didn't disappoint him when she scowled.

"Why must you continue using that ridiculous nickname? I'm not hungry. Go away." She waved her hand, dismissing him and picked up a paint brush.

It was then he noticed how pale she was, the dark circles under her eyes. Placing a hand on her shoulder, he asked, "Are you feeling okay?"

She shrugged him off, irritation lacing her voice as she replied without pausing in brandishing the bright blue paint onto the canvas. "You're not my doctor anymore, remember? You ditched me, so you don't get to ask about my health."

"It's not ethical to sleep with a patient," he returned, his cool rebuke drawing a flush over her face that looked better than the fatigue. That hadn't been his main concern at the time but acknowledging his deeper feelings didn't negate that motive.

A chagrined wince crossed her face. "I didn't think of that." The doorbell chimed and she flicked him a rueful glance, arching her head back. "That's the pizza I ordered. I hope you like the works. It's already paid for."

Mitchell pivoted to go back inside, tossing over his shoulder, "Evasive truths are the same as lying and have consequences. I'll get it."

"Saying I'm not hungry when I am doesn't count," she argued to his back.

Lillian's buttocks clenched at that threat regardless of his mild tone. Needing a few minutes to get herself together, she soaked her brushes and brought her supplies inside, putting everything in the spare bedroom. She heard Mitchell talking to the delivery person then the front door close as she strolled into his bedroom. Upon exploring the house after she returned from a shopping trip into Billings, she discovered the kitchen wasn't the only room in the middle of a renovation. The second bathroom was stripped to the studs, leaving the master bath her only choice.

Her eyes went to the king size bed as she started across the room, the objects lying on the navy comforter halting her in her tracks with a heated stare. She took two steps closer before Mitchell appeared in the door, her nipples puckering in defiance of the rest of her going hot and then cold. Pointing, she demanded to know, "What is that?" She recognized the anal dildo, just not the other, odd thingy that was giving her conniptions.

"A vibrating butt plug." An amused brow winged up as he gave her a bland look.

She released an exasperated breath. "The other thing. And you're so not putting that fat object up my butt."

"You liked the anal beads," he reminded her.

Unable to deny that logic, she drew a breath for patience and replied slowly, "Those were a lot smaller and you took me by surprise. What is that wheel with pointed spokes?"

Walking over to the bed, he picked up the item that popped up goosebumps along her arms with one look, and not the good kind. "It's an e-stim pinwheel. Don't worry, I know how to use it safely, and where. Pizza's getting cold."

Electrical stimulation? A shiver went through her. It was unfair how good he was at stirring her curiosity and lust with a few words accompanied by one of those intent looks.

"Same goes for the plug. There's an enema under the bathroom sink, if that's a concern," he tossed out casually.

Lillian didn't embarrass easily, but the matter-of-fact way he said that made her face burn. Spinning around, she went into the bathroom and slammed the door, the deep rumble of his laugh defusing her abashed indignation. She'd just stepped under the hot spray of one showerhead in the spacious marbled shower when she heard the door open. Peering through the smokey glass, she watched Mitchell walk in and start undressing.

Her pulse jumped as he joined her, all six-foot-four inches of naked, lean muscled male, and she went damp with wanting him, whether he was right for her or not. "I thought you were hungry for food first." She cast a pointed glance at his jutting erection.

Wrapping a hand around his cock, he stroked up and then down as he closed the shower door behind him and moved up to her. "I am, which is why I'm here to speed you along." Reaching up with his free hand, he turned the spray to the side and picked up the soap, crowding her so close her back bumped the wall and his chest hair tickled her nipples.

Steam billowed around them as he released his brick-hard flesh and soaped his hands. There were definitely benefits to their new living arrangement, Lillian contemplated as he ran his sudsy palms over her breasts. "We're going to be in here longer if you keep that up."

"Not much longer. You have such sensitive nipples." He pulled on the soapy buds, elongating her nipples before releasing them with a plop.

Leaning her head back, she closed her eyes and let him have his way until he soaped her pubic curls then lifted her right leg, placing her foot on the corner seat. Lillian opened her eyes to watch him pick up a razor and recalled seeing several women at the club with shaved mounds, wondering what the draw was. It seemed more of a hassle than beneficial, but if that's what he wanted before moving this along, she wouldn't argue.

"I can do it. All you had to do was tell me." She reached to take the razor from his hand but he held it out of her reach with a shake of his head.

"I know you can, but not this time."

She narrowed her eyes but that implacable stare never wavered. "Has anyone ever said no to you?" she grumbled with an exasperated breath.

"My mother, and you. Hold still. I don't want to nick you."

Lillian braced her hands on his shoulders, reminding him, "I despise arrogant men."

"You're sounding like a broken record, pet." Mitchell didn't look up as he swiped the razor through the suds, removing a patch of red curls. Tightening her hands on his shoulders, she thought about kicking him until he drawled, "I wouldn't if I were you."

"God, I hate that you can read me so well. All this fuss. Can't we just have sex?"

"It'll be worth it. Besides, I like to play." He removed another swath and then another before running a finger over the newly bared skin, shocking her with the intense sensations that light touch unleashed.

"Holy shit!" she exclaimed.

He did glance up then, his damp hair clinging to his neck, his eyes sparking with amusement. "You should know by now how well I know women's bodies." His gaze turned serious, his look intense as he stated, "Stick with me, Lillian, and I'll make sure you won't regret it."

Lillian wasn't sure how much he meant by that statement, but the thrill that warmed her chest and curled her toes proved how effectively he had wormed his way past her guard. "I-I might have to give that some thought, Doc."

"You do that. In the meantime, pizza's getting cold."

Mitchell tested her endurance as he finished ridding her of every pubic hair covering her labia and sprinkled between her buttocks. She was so turned on by the time he finished, she almost exploded in climax when he aimed the shower spray on her exposed, tender flesh and ran his hand from front to back, wiping away the suds. She jerked her hips, trying to press against his palm for relief, but he pulled back and turned off the shower before the tiny pulses inside her pussy could take wing and send her flying.

She opened her mouth to protest only to have him cover her lips with a stern rebuke. "One complaint and I'll show you how painful orgasm denial can be. Now," he dropped his hand and opened the shower door, "come on. I'm hungry."

Since that threat lacked the same promise of titillation as a spanking, she buttoned her lips and let him engulf her in a large towel. "That's my girl," he murmured with a wicked gleam in his eyes as he rubbed her briskly from shoulders to feet and she remained silent. He tugged her out of the bathroom and she vowed to get the upper hand at one of these encounters someday soon.

Mitchell saw her take in the pizza box on the bed next to the anal dildo, but she kept quiet and he would bet she was plotting to get even, somehow, someday. He looked forward to her trying. "Bend over so I can insert the plug," he ordered, sliding his hands to press between her shoulders. Those dark eyes flared and her lips tightened before curling in a taunting smile as she braced her hands on the bed.

"Was it my threat that turned you so compliant?" he asked, picking up the already lubed toy and then spreading her cheeks.

"Nope. I'm hungry too." To his surprise, she flipped open the box and picked up a slice of pizza while leaning on her other hand.

Amused, he chuckled, pushing the plug past the tight resistance of her sphincter as she took a bite, chewing slowing with low hums of pleasure as he worked the vibrator inside her. She'd just taken a second bite as he gave that last inch a hard push, the fully embedded toy shaking her enough she wheezed, trying to swallow.

"You're not going to choke on me, are you?" He helped her up and handed her one of the sodas he'd brought in with the pizza.

Red-faced, she gulped it down, her eyes watering as she shuffled her feet. "That was uncalled for," she growled, handing him back the can.

"I don't think so." Turning her toward the bed, he patted her butt. "Climb up and sit at the headboard."

He followed her onto the bed, enjoying the sway of her plugged ass as she crawled to the pillows and turned over. Settling at the foot of the bed, he placed the pizza between them and grabbed a large piece. "*Mmmm*, good. Thanks for dinner."

Her slim brows dipped into a confused frown. "We're just going to sit here naked and eat?"

He shrugged. "Sure. Why not?" Taking another bite, he watched her expression go from baffled to stupefied to mortified with his deepened voice and order to, "Bend your knees and spread your legs." He held up a hand against the swift protest crossing her face. "Remember the consequences I mentioned in the shower."

Sitting back, Lillian followed his command and spread her bent knees, offering him a lovely view of her glistening pink slit and the flat end of the dildo nestled between her buttocks. "Between your patients and the women you've tormented over the years, haven't you seen enough naked bodies?"

"The female body fascinates me, as does the different responses I can pull from the same touch or scene. Are you ready to tell me why you stayed with your ex until your sister died? How long were you with him?" Her jaw went rigid and he could see in her glaring eyes she didn't want to talk about the man. Too bad. If he intended to pursue this relationship, which he wanted to, he needed to know what McCabe had held over her to keep her with him. That was the only explanation why a woman like Lillian would stick with an abusive ass.

"How long were you married? Did she obey your every dictate every time you snapped your fingers?" she countered.

Fair is fair, Mitchell decided, reaching for another slice of pizza. He rarely talked about Abbie; at first because it was too painful, and after moving here because he was trying to put the past to bed and start over. Lillian deserved to hear a few details about his last relationship as much as he did hers.

"Fair enough," he replied after swallowing. "We were married one year after we met, together eight years. And yes, she was submissive to the bone and not only obeyed my commands without question but relished my control. Abbie was the complete opposite of you."

"Makes me wonder even more what I'm doing here, with you," she murmured.

"If it helps, I'm just as baffled by it."

Lillian blew out a breath, glanced out the window for a few silent moments and then faced him with a resigned expression. She appeared to either have forgotten her exposed position or had become so comfortable with it, it no longer embarrassed her.

"I dated Brad for a few weeks before his control issues became unbearable." A quick grin came and went on her face as she said, "I broke up with him, telling him bossy, control freaks weren't my type."

"And yet, here you are, with me."

"Yeah. Go figure. You're nothing like him, though. I can't picture you threatening a comatose woman to get someone back in your bed."

That son of a bitch. Mitchell went taut with anger as he imagined Lillian's terror for her sister. He didn't need her to tell him how close the two of them were, he'd seen it reflected on her sorrowful face numerous times. "The morning she died you were free of that threat." That was easy to deduce, and another wrenching heartbreak for her to cope with, he imagined.

"Yes. It was awful, the grief mixing up with relief." She sighed, took a long drink of soda and then said, "I took off, went by the bank and just drove."

Picking up the e-stim pinwheel, Mitchell leaned forward and wrapped a hand around her right ankle, bringing her foot to his lap as he confessed, "I went up to our cabin and stayed drunk for a week. My mother and sister came up and dragged me back."

Flicking the stimulator on low, he ran the spiked wheel along the bottom of her foot, watching her tear-filled eyes dry as surprised arousal took over. "You have no other family?"

She shook her head, dropping the crust left from her pizza onto the bed and gripping the comforter in her fists. "No, it had been just the two of us for several years."

That explained even more of her story and sorrow. He couldn't imagine having to cope without his family's support. "Well, now you have new relationships. You should think about staying, cultivating them, give them a chance to fill the void in your life." He rolled the instrument around her ankle, over the top of her foot and slowly up the inside of her leg.

"Right now I can't think about anything except what you're doing," she breathed, her nipples puckering into tighter pinpoints the closer he got to her pussy. She lifted her eyes from his traveling hand to his face, her breath catching as she demanded, "You wouldn't, would you?"

"What do you think?"

"Oh, God, you would."

Lillian shuddered as the light buzzing and tiny pinpricks neared the sensitive apex where her thigh met hip, her mind switching gears back to her decadent vulnerable position. Mitchell's eyes, more green than brown now, traveled from her face, down her chest to rest on her exposed vagina, and damn if she didn't relish his heated stare at her most intimate body part. The plug's vibrations distracted her from the discomforting full sensation and she ached for a touch, any touch on her clit.

"See how well you know me already?" She held her breath as he circled around her gaping folds and over her denuded mound.

She squealed as those vibrations and pricks unleashed a torrent of new sensations from nerve endings never exposed before. Before she could beg him to stop, it was too much, he slid upward, across her quivering belly and lightly around the fleshy mound of her left breast. Her stalled breathing quickened, her pulse skyrocketing as he bent his head and licked her right nipple while circling her left bud with the torturing device. Tingles from the stimulation buzzed under her skin as he pushed harder on the pointed spikes, just enough to sting and leave small red dots in its wake.

"Mitchell," she groaned, wondering if she wanted him to torture her nipple or move away.

"I'll decide," he stated, as if he read her mind again. Covering her nipple with his hot mouth, he trailed the pinwheel over the other, the combination of vibrations deep inside her tissues and painful jabs into the tender nub dragging a shriek past her tight throat. Her legs quivered, sweat broke out along her body and her hips bucked, her needy pussy begging for attention.

With a low curse, he tossed the pinwheel aside, reared up to grip her hair and tilt her head back for a hard, deep kiss as he sheathed his cock with his free hand. "Why is it," he ground out, sitting back on his heels and then lifting her onto his steely erection, "it's always hard and fast with you?"

"I don't know, don't care." She moaned as he pulled her down, cramming his cock inside her as she clutched his sides with her bent knees. Between the dildo and his thick shaft, she'd never felt so full, the tight fit uncomfortable until he reached behind her and removed the plug. She breathed easier until he grabbed her hips, lifted and then slammed her back down with a guttural command.

"Ride me, pet."

Gripping his shoulders, she bounced on his cock, his heavy grunts mingling with her mewling whimpers as he drove into her over and over. The bed squeaked, her breasts bounced and their lower bodies slapped together in the fast race to completion that left them both winded and shaking from the onslaught of drenching ecstasy.

Chapter 12

"How big is this place?" Lillian asked as Mitchell drove through the open gates leading onto Kurt's ranch.

"I don't know the exact acreage but it's one of the largest in the state. I'm going to check in on Leland, Kurt's father, while you and Leslie visit. We'll come find you when I'm through." He pulled to a stop in front of a sprawling ranch home, complete with a wide front porch and rocking chairs facing several barns of varying sizes across a spacious lawn.

Lillian hopped out of the SUV and took in the sweeping view of miles and miles of open prairie expanding beyond her vision. She spotted groups of grazing black cattle and cowboys riding the herds with expert horsemanship she admired, clusters of wooded areas and an island range in the far distance. Wildflowers and greener grasses could be spotted here and there, signs an early spring was right around the corner. She inhaled a lungful of fresh air and listened to the neigh of horses prancing in a large corral behind one of the barns.

She'd always thought Salt Lake City was a medium sized city, not too big or too small, with all the amenities and social activities she needed to keep her happy there. Now, compared to

Willow Springs surrounded by all of this land free of large buildings, busy traffic and the clamor of city noise, her hometown held less appeal.

Mitchell came around and took her hand, cocking his head as he asked, "What are you pondering over so seriously?"

She shook her head, offering him a smile as the front door opened and an attractive woman with long, sandy blonde hair and bright blue eyes came out to greet them. "Just comparing this to home. Cows and horses instead of cars, weird."

"It grows on you. Come meet Leslie."

"Hey, Doc. Go on in, I'll take Lillian on a tour," Leslie said as she skipped down the porch steps with her hand outstretched toward Lillian.

"I'd like that." Lillian shook her hand and waved to Mitchell as Leslie steered her toward the corral.

"Okay, he's inside. Give me the scoop. I've only heard tidbits." The gleam in Leslie's eyes and expectant look reminded Lillian of Nan and Avery's initial reactions when they had first met her.

"Let's just say I never held an interest in the lifestyle you've enjoyed for a while until I met him. He's had a way of changing my mind about a few things. Oh, aren't you sweet?" Lillian rubbed the silky nose of a miniature horse trotting up to the rail.

"That's Taffy. You wouldn't know it to look at her now, but six months ago her ribs were showing and she'd lost a lot of her hair due to malnutrition. Kurt surprised me with her and her brother." Leslie nodded toward another small pony across the paddock. "It was love at first sight. Isn't that right, sweetie?"

Taffy abandoned Lillian for Leslie, butting her head against her owner's arm.

Leslie held her hand out, palm flat, offering the mare a sugar cube. "She takes that so politely," Lillian stated, in awe of the little horse's affection for her mistress. Because she traveled a lot for art shows, she'd never owned a pet but used to 'dog sit'

Liana's scruffy little mixed breed that had been cute as a button. They were both devastated when Brandy died of heart failure at age thirteen.

Leslie glanced at her, asking, "Something wrong?"

"Just thinking about my sister and a dog she used to have. Adorable little thing, and the closest I've come to a pet."

Lifting her hand in a wave to one of the ranch hands galloping by, Leslie replied, "It didn't take me long to fall in love with these two and I didn't have any experience with horses. Kurt, and several of the guys around here all gave me pointers and help when I needed it. I'm sorry about your sister. I think it was Avery who told me she passed away recently."

"Yes, a month ago. Sometimes it seems longer than that, and sometimes like it was just yesterday. Those horses are beautiful." She pointed toward the second barn and the regal heads hanging out the open, upper doors of their stalls.

"Those are the Thoroughbreds for breeding and sale. I'll show you." Hopping off the rail, Lillian followed her toward the stable, surprised when Leslie said, "I went four years without seeing or speaking to my older sister after I was put into the witness protection program, so I can sympathize, to a degree, with how you must feel. I was devastated without contact with my only family."

"Now it's my turn to say give me the scoop. How did you end up in witness protection?" The scent of sweet hay and pungent manure hit her nostrils as they entered the neatly kept stables. Even in the dimmer lighting, she could see the sorrow crossing Leslie's face at her question.

"I witnessed a murder, a nice man who never hurt anyone. They were spoiled, punk teens, riding high on drugs and unafraid of consequences due to their father always bailing them out. I didn't realize how far he would go to protect his kids, or how much I would have to give up when my testimony sent the boys to prison and he threatened me." She reached up to stroke a hand down the sleek neck of a black equine. "Keeping to myself so I wouldn't inadvertently put anyone else at risk should he ever find me was the hardest after missing my sister."

They strolled down the clean-swept aisle with large stalls on each side, the tremor of remembered heartbreak in Leslie's hushed voice drawing on Lillian's sympathy. "That was quite a sacrifice on your part. Was it worth it?"

Leslie stopped at the stall of a huge stallion, his muscles rippling as he pawed at his door. "Kurt rescued this guy from the dog food factory. He was a mean son-of-a-bitch, unrideable and malnourished. My fiancé busted his butt gaining his trust and getting him healthy again and I lost track of how many times I asked him if he was worth it." Reaching a steady hand toward the animal, she rubbed behind one ear, unafraid. "He would always reply 'ask me again later', but as you can see, I didn't need to. Devil here is still feisty but happy and healthy, and worth every sweaty, painful hour Kurt put in working with him. Yes, Lillian, as hard as those four years away from my sister and home were, it was worth it to see justice for Alessandro. Come on." She nudged her with her elbow and a smile. "It's too nice an afternoon to brood about the past. There's the cutest premature calf I want to show you. I'm trying to convince Kurt to let me keep her."

Laughing in disbelief, she followed Leslie outside, asking, "Why?"

"Because otherwise she'll end up on someone's table and I helped bottle feed that baby."

"Oh, well, when put that way, it makes sense."

Leslie grinned. "I like you, Lillian. Kurt didn't think so, but I almost have him agreeing."

Lillian enjoyed the hour she spent alone with Leslie, listening to her talk about her second-grade students with such fondness, how her relationship with Kurt had begun with a one-night stand between two strangers and meeting several young cowpokes whose polite addresses tickled her. After she crooned over the tiny calf with big doe eyes, they strolled across the lawn and up a small hill, walking by the family plot, shaded by large trees, the graves decorated with plants and fresh cut, colorful flowers. The story of how Kurt lost both his mother and sister so close together resurrected the sorrow of her own losses.

"I'm sorry," Leslie said, reaching over to squeeze her hand. "I wasn't thinking. It's become a ritual for me to come up here and check on the plants and flowers when Babs, our housekeeper and cook, has the day off."

Shaking her head, Lillian turned away from Leslie's sympathetic gaze. "It's all right. Everyone has lost someone, right?"

"True, but that doesn't make it any easier." Pivoting, Leslie led the way toward another corral where Lillian saw Mitchell and Kurt saddling three horses.

"That's a beautiful horse," she remarked, nodding toward the pale-coated stallion Kurt was tossing a saddle onto.

"That's Atlas and he's a sweetie. Not as sweet as my girl, Anna Leigh. She's the Appaloosa between Atlas and Mitchell's bay."

Mitchell looked up as they approached, his gaze as probing as always, Lillian's response to it the same with warm tingles racing across her skin. With his Stetson shading his face, the sleeves of his black western shirt rolled to below his elbows, those long, muscled legs encased in snug denim and wearing scuffed boots, he appeared more a rough wrangler than a medical professional. Either way, her heart tripped as he held a hand out to her and she wondered what pivoting point in their relationship had caused her to set aside her annoyance with his autocratic tendencies long enough to fall for the protective, caring side of him.

"You're thinking too hard, pet" he whispered in her ear as she took his hand.

"I have to around you," she retorted before turning to smile at Kurt. "Thank you for inviting me out today. I've had fun touring your ranch with Leslie."

"It's good to see you again, Lillian. The tour's just begun. Mount up with Mitchell and I'll show you some of the prettiest country in Montana."

She could see why Leslie had fallen for the cattleman as she watched him boost his fiancée onto the dainty mare. Dressed similar to Mitchell only wearing a burgundy shirt, he sported a perpetual five o'clock shadow along his jaw that was as dark as his black hair and ebony eyes. Lillian sure hoped things worked out between her and Mitchell because there would be no going back to the pansy, vanilla lovers she used to date after being subjected to the focused gazes and sexual dominance of these cowboys.

"You're up with me, Leslie." Mitchell's gruff voice pulled her head out of the clouds and she turned to see him mounted and leaning down with an outstretched hand. "Don't worry, Phantom's well trained now."

"What do you mean now?" She clasped his hand before she could let the size of the animal scare her off. With little effort, he swung her up and wrapped a tight arm around her waist as she settled astride in front of him, surprised the horse didn't budge.

Kurt sent her a wicked grin, turning his steed around to face them. "I thought he was crazy to pick that son-of-a-bitch at auction last year, but Doc swore he saw something in his eyes that made him worth saving. For a city bloke, it turns out he has a good eye for horseflesh. We're heading east."

"I know a good bet when I see one," Mitchell said, his arm tightening around her waist as he kicked the horse into a slow walk.

Leslie gripped his forearm, refusing to look down. From the distance she could now see, she knew how high up they sat. The slow, sedate pace lulled her into relaxing and leaning back against that wide, rock-solid chest, the deep rumble of Mitchell's voice above her a pleasure to listen to. The never-ending acres of fields were broken up by wooded areas and in the distance they pointed out a mountain range that appeared as an island of higher ground and would make an awesome painting.

"Oh, I wish I thought to grab my camera." She sighed wistfully as her mind filled with potential art.

"You'll have to come back when spring is in full bloom," Kurt said. "There's nothing prettier than the prairies in the warmer months."

She could tell he loved the ranch from his proud tone, and Lillian envied him that connection to a special place. Would she still be here in two months? God help her, she hoped so. Right now, she wanted nothing more than to see where her relationship with Mitchell could lead.

Kurt pulled to a stop, glancing at Mitchell. "I'm going to check on the west pasture. Why don't you show Leslie the falls and we'll meet up with you there before heading back? I'll put steaks on when we return."

"Sounds good. About an hour?"

"That'll work."

"You'll love the waterfall copse, Lillian. See you there." Leslie waved as they nudged their horses into a gallop and took off, leaving her alone with Mitchell, the late afternoon sun warming her face as she turned to look up at him.

"It's just you and me now. Are you ready to ride?" he asked, his breath wafting over her lips.

Oh, yeah, but probably not in the way he meant. More than the afternoon temperature was warming her now, and as he kicked Phantom into a butt-bouncing trot and then let him out in a full run across the meadow, more than the breeze and exhilarating ride were stirring her senses into high alert. The clomp of hooves pounding the ground, her squeals of delight and his low chuckles as they raced toward a row of trees echoed in the air. They were panting by the time he slowed down and entered the cooler shade of the woods at a brisk walk, winding along a wide path until they entered a secluded clearing.

"It's beautiful," she breathed, taking in the rushing stream that flowed over a small rise and emptied into a clear as glass pond, with an artist's eye. "That's why Leslie called it the waterfall copse."

"Yes." Dismounting, he reached up and lifted her down. "The first time I took Phantom out of the corral, we rode here. It's peaceful."

She gave him a sharp look, trying to detect what that note was behind his soft voice. As usual, his face revealed nothing of what he was thinking, and she found that as frustrating as the easy way he had of reading her every expression. Wanting to distract them both, she toed off her sneakers, asking, "Is it cold?"

"Frigid. You don't want to do that, Lillian," he warned as she bent to pull off her socks.

"Says who?" Skipping out of his reach, she laughed and dashed to the pond's edge, getting a face full of cold misting spray from the splashing falls. Shivering but undeterred, she stuck her feet in and then jumped back out again with a squeal. "Okay, you were right."

"Of course. Walk around some so your muscles don't tighten up on you since you're not used to riding."

That smug reply followed by yet another order reminded her of her plans to turn the tables on him just once. She faced him to see him leaning against a tree, keeping his distance while watching her from under the brim of his hat. In that moment, she longed more than anything to bring a look of stunned surprise followed by pleasure to his face, the same as he'd managed with her numerous times.

Giddy excitement turned her palms damp and set her heart to racing as she sauntered toward him, a small smile curling her lips as she decided what she would do. "You know, *Master* Mitchell, I've never been naked outdoors, but I bet you have." Whipping off her top over her head, she dropped it on the ground and reached for the front clasp of her bra. She was prepared for him to jump in and take over as she shrugged off her bra, but instead he gave her a moment's pause with his unexpected, stern reply.

"We don't have time to play today. Get dressed, Lillian."

His gaze raked her bare breasts, her nipples turning to pinpoints from the cool breeze and his hot eyes, but he made no move toward her. Not one to give up on a plan once she put it into motion, she lowered her zipper and shimmied out of her jeans and panties, pasting on a bland, innocent expression as she asked, "Why not? We have almost an hour." A shiver danced down her spine from the exposure to open air and his rigid stance. Goosebumps broke out as she moved toward him, even as liquid heat flooded her pussy.

Uh, oh. His jaw went taut and his nostrils flared as he growled, "I mean it. This isn't what I planned today, so get dressed."

Okay, that sealed it. It was time to show him he didn't always get to call the shots. Besides, she was having fun switching things around for once. "No."

"Excuse me?"

"*Mmmm.*" Reaching him, she had his belt unbuckled and her fingers on his zipper tab before he knew it. "I'll think about it. Meanwhile, you should be still or I might pinch you." His erection pressed against the metal tabs as she slowly lowered it. He must have read the intent on her face because he sucked in a deep breath until his cock sprang free and landed in her hands. And then he swore.

"Fuck, pet, you're going to pay for this," he ground out as she sank to her knees.

Probably. But as she took him in her mouth, for the first time that threat didn't faze her. With a ray of sunlight warming her back and butt, one hard hand braced on her shoulder, the other kneading her breast, all she cared about was giving him pleasure for a change and denying him his way for once. Gripping the base of his cock, she took him deep, swirling her tongue around his steely girth, suckling his hardness with her lips and cheeks.

Birds trilled overhead, the rush of water came from behind her and his harsh breathing blew hot on top of her head as she tickled the delicate underside of his crown. She smiled around his shaft as he jerked, nibbling along the ridged veins as she shifted her free hand to palm his heavy sac. He only gave her another minute to toy with him before clasping her face and holding her still while he took over. She wasn't surprised but never dreamed the carnality of being held immobile while he fucked her mouth could be such a turn-on.

A moan slid up her throat as Mitchell pumped inside her mouth with short jabs and a guttural demand. "You started this, now finish it. Suck me hard, pet."

Lillian quivered, hollowing her cheeks and giving him what he wanted, what he demanded. Rolling his balls in her hand, she reached between her spread knees with the other and slid her fingers between her slick folds. *Suck, stroke, suck, stroke*, she hummed inside her head, relishing the stretch of her mouth and taste of him seeping onto her tongue. He pulled back and she lapped over his seeping slit as she toyed with her clit. As he shoved back inside deep enough to bump her throat, she jammed her fingers far enough to touch her womb. She mewled around his hard flesh and gyrated against her palm. Her jaw grew sore, her hand tired and then he was spewing his cum down her throat as her climax soaked her pumping fingers.

By the time he released her to fall back on her heels, shaking from the experience, the sound of horses approaching reached her ears.

Disgusted with his lack of control, Mitchell zipped up and helped Lillian stand. Damn it, he'd planned to show her today how much he enjoyed her company even without sex, but he couldn't turn her down after he saw the gleam in her eyes that hinted she was testing him in some way. Did she instigate and push this scene because she needed to prove to herself she hadn't given him complete control over her, or was it just to surprise him with the role reversal? Either way, he couldn't let her down any more than he could keep from taking over. Now, looking into her sated eyes and at the pleased smile playing around those soft lips, he was glad he'd set aside the urge to insist on sticking with his original plan.

Giving her a quick, hard kiss, he swatted her ass hard enough to burn. "Grab your clothes and get dressed. All of a sudden I'm starving for that steak Kurt mentioned." With a laugh that drew his smile, she snatched up her jeans and was pulling her top over her head when Kurt and Leslie rode up.

Mitchell pulled into his drive Friday afternoon, his heart executing a familiar slow roll when he saw Lillian's Mazda in the garage. Was it just six weeks ago when she'd landed in a snowdrift and interrupted his retreat? Despite his irritation with her involuntary intrusion on his pity party, her own loss and grief coupled with that backbone of sheer grit had somehow wormed its way past his defenses. She was nothing like Abbie, or any of the submissive women he had hooked up with before he married or after his wife's death. And yet, he mused, at this time in his life, he discovered she was just right for him, whom he needed and wanted going forward. The hows and whys didn't matter, he figured, sliding out of his vehicle and striding up to the front door. Only that he could convince her they had something going between them that was good enough to warrant exploring further.

Entering the house, he veered toward the living room, wishing his first on-call shift at the Billings hospital didn't start this evening. He would have liked to pour himself a drink before coaxing her into talking about staying. Instead, he went to the fireplace and lifted Abbie's picture down, experiencing that little tug of nostalgia he always felt when he looked at her smiling face.

She would always own a small corner of his heart, he didn't and wouldn't deny that to himself or Lillian. But, as he'd discovered these past weeks, his heart was big enough to love two special women, each in their own, different way.

Lillian heard Mitchell come in and added a few more strokes to her current painting before setting aside her paintbrush to greet him. With her hair pulled up and dressed in the long, flaring skirt she had bought to replace the one damaged in the fire and one of her paint-smeared tee shirts, she pondered changing first then squashed that idea. He'd seen her in similar disarray almost every day. Nervous anticipation rolled through her as she stood. She'd spent the morning in town, first opening an account at the bank and then having lunch with Nan and Avery, telling them of her plans to stick around for the foreseeable future. They'd been as thrilled as she'd been nervous, and she ended up leaving her jacket at the teashop.

Every time she thought of moving on, she couldn't think of anywhere she would rather be, or people she would rather get to know better. After sleeping curled next to Mitchell every night this past week, her body still humming from his demanding possession every morning, her heart pounding from more than the sweeping ecstasy, the thought of being alone again turned her cold. He hadn't said in so many words he wanted her to stay, and if she'd read him wrong and he didn't want her to continue staying with him after the apartment repairs were finished, she wasn't sure what she would do, where she would go from here. She was praying she wasn't wrong.

Padding barefoot inside, she came around the corner to the living room, the giddy rush to see him turning to a gut-clenching wave of despair as she spotted him staring at Abbie's picture on the fireplace mantle. The look on his face dashed her hopes that they could make something of their odd pairing, cutting her off at the knees. The profound love etched in every line of his face revealed how deeply he had cared for his wife, a submissive woman eager and willing to do his bidding day and night. And that wasn't her. She'd grown to embrace and benefit from his sexual dominance, something she still struggled to accept, but she wouldn't, couldn't give him complete say so over her life. The month she'd lived under Brad's thumb and demands had been the most difficult weeks of her life, and not just because of his threats against Liana and her sister's hopeless condition.

I've been such an idiot. How could she hope to compete with what he'd shared with Abbie? She didn't expect him to gaze at her with such an expression of devotion so soon in their relationship, but she was such a complete opposite of Abbie, of what he really wanted in a significant other, how could she hope he might come to care for her just as deeply? She must have made a sound because his head swiveled toward the door and he beckoned her forward.

"Why are you hovering over there? Come here." He placed the picture back on the mantle and held his hand out to her.

She walked toward him, her heart thundering in her ears, stopping out of his reach and ignoring his hand as she looked at the picture. "You loved her very much." Her voice wobbled but she didn't care.

"Yes, I did. Something wrong, pet?"

Something snapped inside Lillian at hearing Mitchell call her that nickname, the one she'd switched from hating to liking and now, back to hating again. *How dare he utter that endearment in that caressing tone seconds after mourning his one and only love?* Lifting her arm, she knocked his hand aside as he reached out to her, stepping back with an icy glare.

"If you can't respect my wishes regarding that degrading epithet then don't talk to me."

His lips tightened and he fisted his hands on his hips, giving her a glacial stare she refused to back down from. "If you have a problem, *Lillian*, tell me and we'll talk about it."

God, she despised the sneer in his voice when he said her name. "No problem, just asking for some of that respect you're always demanding in return."

She could tell he didn't believe her and his words confirmed it. "Bullshit. What's… *fuck*." He grabbed his buzzing phone off the mantle, answering with a curt, "Doctor Hoffstetter."

Lillian wasn't disappointed when he replied to the caller, "I'm on my way," and hung up. "Wouldn't you know it? A trauma case is on its way into All Saints, a car accident. I have to go. We'll finish this when I get back." He started out, swung around, hauled her against him and ravaged her mouth in a kiss that left her shaken, needy and desperate to leave before she made a complete fool of herself.

Bryan watched the doctor walk out of his house and drive away just twenty minutes after arriving home, hoping against hope his chance to rifle through Lillian's car for her camera was finally near. His patience in sitting here, biding his time for an opportunity to move fast without detection had been wearing thin. When he noticed she had started parking in the garage, he almost changed his mind and headed back to Utah empty handed. He had given himself a few more days, tonight being the last, before admitting defeat.

During the day, Lillian was either running around town or left the car in the drive, making it too risky to search it with neighbors so close by. At night, with the doctor in residence and her car locked in the garage, he hesitated to make a move under the new spotlights installed this week. But now, with dusk falling and Hoffstetter leaving with the garage door still open, his luck might be turning.

Casting a furtive scan of the street as he got out of his car, he followed the same route through the neighbor's back yards to the rear of the doctor's garage and sidled along the side and in through the open door, crouching until he reached the door handle on the passenger side of the Mazda. Putting his cigarette in his mouth, he breathed a sigh of relief when he found it unlocked. "Bingo," he whispered, snatching the camera out of the glove compartment and backing out.

A startled gasp behind him drew a low curse as he spun around to see Brad's ex staring at him wide-eyed, a suitcase in each hand.

"Bryan? What are you doing?" Her gaze went to the camera in his hand, her eyes going to narrow slits of suspicion. "What the hell are you doing with my camera?"

"*Fuck!*" Striding forward, he gripped her arm, his only thought to get out of there before the doctor returned. As he dragged her toward the back, he saw the moment she put two and two together and faced the fact there was no going back now. Her face paled as she dropped the bags and struggled in his hold.

Lillian shoved her fear aside as enlightenment dawned with the whiff of cigarette smoke. Swinging her free arm back, she slapped Bryan's face with as much strength as she could muster, knocking the cigarette from his mouth. "You broke in upstairs and caused that fire." She pulled against his bruising grip, digging in her feet as he kept going. "Damn it, why? Let me go!" she cried out.

Whirling on her, he drew a gun from behind his waist and pressed it against her temple with a snarl. "Shut up and move."

Terror overruled her anger and she went with him, praying for an intervention before they got far. This had to do with his brother, there was no other explanation. But... *shit*. "It's the pictures you're after, isn't it?" she panted as they reached a car parked around the corner. "You're protecting that bastard again, aren't you?"

Opening the driver's door, he shoved her in ahead of him and she scooted as far away from him as the other door allowed. Going for the handle, she swore when it didn't budge and he took off before she could unlock it, speeding down the residential street like a bat out of hell.

Grabbing hold for safety, she glared at him and repeated, "Aren't you?"

"Yes," he snapped, running a nervous hand through his hair.

Before she could say anything else, he took the next corner with a squeal of tires, throwing her against the door as she saw Nan passing them, likely on her way to Mitchell's house to return her jacket. Lillian had just enough time to mouth 'help' and prayed it would be enough.

Nan slammed on the brakes, turned around and memorized the license plate on the car before pulling over. Grabbing her phone, the image of Lillian's frantic face as that man sped by giving her heart palpitations, she muttered, "Come on, come on, pick up… Grayson, oh, thank God." She rushed to tell him what she'd just witnessed, rattling off the license plate number.

"I'm on it. Get hold of Dan and Mitchell."

The sheriff's brusque, no-nonsense tone eased Nan's trembling as she hung up and called Mitchell and then her husband.

What the hell? Mitchell was halfway to Billings when the hospital called to tell him the victim was D.O.A. and he was no longer needed. He'd barely had time to regret the unexpected death when his phone buzzed again, and Nan's news turned his blood ice-cold. Whipping around, he sped back down the highway as he put in a call to Grayson on speaker. "Talk to me, damn it," he demanded as soon as his friend answered.

"He has to be headed out of town and the highway is our best bet. I've put out an APB and abduction alert. We'll get him.

If you and I and my backup don't block him on the highway, someone will spot them and pull him over."

Grayson gave him a description of the car and Mitchell vowed to do something special for Nan when this was over. Right now, all he could think about was Lillian's safety. Losing her was not an option.

Chapter 13

"This is all your fault, you know." Bryan sent her an angry glare as he hit the highway at an accelerated speed.

"How so?" Lillian worked at taking deep breaths to keep her nerves from screaming. She was trusting Nan to get help, praying a law enforcement vehicle spotted them soon. "Your brother is the one who threatened my sister and knocked me around. You're the one who broke into my apartment and car, I'm assuming to swipe the evidence I have of Saint Brad's handiwork," she sneered.

His perspiration-damp brow furrowed as he snarled, "What the fuck are you talking about, threatened your sister? She's dead."

Those blunt words caused her heart to constrict but she concentrated on the puzzlement in his tone instead. "You honestly don't have a clue what Brad is capable of, guilty of, do you?" she scoffed. "After breaking up with him because of his control issues, do you honestly think I'd take him back without being coerced? I don't sit in awe of your brother, never had, never will. Only you do, you blind jackass."

Bryan tightened his hands on the steering wheel as his eyes darted back and forth along the highway. "Don't give me that bullshit. He told me how you went nuts when he ended it between you two, how you attacked him and left him with a concussion he damn near died from."

Wincing, she shook her head in disbelief at the lies Brad was capable of. "I didn't know he was hurt that bad. He's the doctor, for God's sake, not me. And he didn't end it, I did when Liana died and he could no longer threaten her with harm if I didn't stay with him. Believe me or not, I don't care. I don't know what you're planning, but you won't…" She broke off as a highway patrol came speeding out of a turnoff and roaring up behind them with sirens wailing. Relief washed through her, bringing a strange calmness in the wake of the danger she was still in. "Pull over, Bryan. You can't… *Oh!*"

Not only did Sheriff Grayson's cruiser join in the chase along with the highway patrol but hordes of riders were barreling across the fields bracketing both sides of the highway, every cowboy armed with a rifle. But as Bryan cursed a blue streak, refusing to slow down, it was the sight of Mitchell's SUV coming at them from the front, followed by several more siren blaring police cars that settled the final dregs of her anxiety. Reaching over, she squeezed Bryan's rigid arm, imploring, "Please, stop. You have to know it's over."

He slowed to a crawl and then stopped, his expression bleak as he pointed his gun at her. "I still have you to get me out of this."

Mitchell came to a careening, sideways halt in front of them as the Dunbar brothers and their cowhands reined in their mounts and aimed their rifles with grim, determined expressions on the left, Kurt Wilcox and his loyal hands riding to the rescue on the right. As drool-worthy, panty-melting a scene as the cowboy posse made, it was the expression on her doctor cowboy's face as he got out and came toward them with his hand stretched toward her that did it for her. *I was an idiot for not trusting him with my heart as much as I did my body.* There was no hiding or denying the fierce protective set to his face or the glint of profound caring in his eyes.

She reached for the door handle, swinging her gaze back to Bryan. "No you don't." Waving her hand around them, she smiled. "You may have been blind about your brother, but you can see what's right in front of you now. Think about it, Bryan. Do you want to be a cop in prison for murder or settle for a plea bargain for kidnapping, which I promise to support?" With a deep breath and shaking hand, she got out of his car and walked toward her future.

Six months later

The sprawling green lawn surrounding Caden Dunbar's home was teeming with the townsfolk of Willow Springs and his ranching neighbors. Two eight-foot-long tables held a buffet of homemade casseroles, salads and desserts, ten other tables offered seating for the picnickers who were enjoying the Dunbar's hospitality at their annual barbeque. Young children were squealing on top of ponies in a makeshift riding ring, teenage boys were hitting baseballs out in a field and several grills were sending plumes of smoke-filled tantalizing aromas into the air. Mitchell leaned against the towering Ponderosa pine at the corner of the lawn, eating an ice cream cone, enjoying the shade against the afternoon September sun and watching Lillian fuss over babies.

A rueful smile curled his lips as Avery strolled over to the blanket carrying their three-month old daughter. As usual, Grayson was keeping an eagle eye on mother and daughter with the occasional glare toward Caden or Connor as a reminder to keep their boys away from his girl. If he kept it up, the sheriff would have more gray hair than Mitchell before the kid hit kindergarten. The five-and-a-half-month-old Dunbar baby boys were rolling around together on the blanket, their mothers, Nan, Leslie, Kelsey and Lillian laughing at their antics.

He had declined the invitation to the picnic last year, having just relocated and was still getting his bearings, but now wished he had attended. Spread out before him lay the picture of a close-knit community, faces of friends who would go that extra mile for you and a woman who had filled the empty void in his life Abbie's passing left behind.

His palms still turned sweaty, his heart racing whenever he thought back to that evening when he'd seen Lillian's pale face staring at him in wondrous disbelief through the windshield of her kidnapper's car. He didn't know how word of her kidnapping had reached their friends and the ranches so fast, but his gratitude remained endless. The way she'd gone to bat for Bryan McCabe, giving her blessing for a reduced sentence, stayed a bone of contention between them. No matter how hard he and Grayson argued against forgiving the man, that stubborn grit of hers took hold and they failed to shake it loose. She'd said she'd seen the moment he had believed her over his brother and regretted his actions, and she wanted nothing more than to put the incident behind her. The ten years he was spending in prison were enough of a punishment on a disgraced cop.

She'd had some explaining to do after they had returned to his house that night and he'd seen her bags packed. That evening had been the first of many open, candid conversations between them and the start of cementing their feelings for each other. Over the summer, he taught her to embrace her sexual submissive side and she, in turn, tried to stay patient whenever he lapsed and got 'bossy' when sex wasn't involved.

Reaching into his pocket, he fingered the ring he brought with him, a peacefulness settling over him as he watched her walk toward him with a small smile that stirred his cock. Yeah, he loved her, enough to tie her to him and hopefully welcome a child of his own into this world within the next year. He held out his hand, noticed several people looking their way, Caden giving him a thumbs up and Connor winking.

It never failed. Lillian's pulse skipped a beat as she took Mitchell's hand and saw that same look on his face as she'd seen when he'd driven up to her rescue six months ago, along with everyone else. They were still in the process of working out the kinks in their relationship, and that would likely continue for some time, being such opposites. But they'd been having a good time rounding out those jagged edges. She stayed up worrying when he would get a late-night trauma call and he didn't complain when he traveled with her to the Taos Summer Art Festival and she had left him on his own to attend her booth. They'd gone rapid river rafting and he'd talked her into having sex on the balcony of the hotel room. There were some perks to shacking up with a man into kinky pleasures.

Over the summer he'd taught her to ride and she'd given him art lessons. He'd shown her how inventive he could get on horseback and how creative he could get with finger paints. They spent a weekend at Devin and Greg's Wild Horse Dude Ranch for their wedding to Kelsey and Lillian loved the trail ride up to the top of the flat hills. Sydney and Tamara were a hoot after imbibing too much wine at Leslie's bridal shower, celebrating their first drink after childbirth. Kurt and Leslie's church wedding in Billings had brought tears to Lillian's eyes.

"What's that shit eating grin for?" Mitchell asked, yanking her against him.

Lillian plucked the cone from his hand, leaning against him as she licked the smooth, cold ice cream. "*Mmmm*, just remembering Taos, and the balcony, and riding back to the falls on Kurt's ranch, and last week, when you brought out the finger paints..."

He lifted a brow. "Want to sneak away into one of the barns and fool around? I'm sure our hosts won't mind."

She huffed a laugh, that familiar thrill sweeping through her at the prospect. "They won't, but their parents and a few other of our town's not-so-open-minded elders might."

"And we don't want to offend anyone."

She shook her head, looking around at the friends whose unconditional support and welcome had slowly eased her loneliness and helped her come to terms with Liana's death. "No, we don't. Funny, isn't it," she murmured, "how we both ended up here, grieving, and found a new home in the process?"

"Fate, kismet, call it whatever you want, I love you, Lillian. Marry me, stay here in Willow Springs with me, grow old with me, and I promise I'll *try* not to be too bossy."

Tossing the cone on the ground, she smirked. "You always did make it hard for me to say no to you, Doc. For better or worse, Willow Springs is home now and you're the one I can't live without."

As Mitchell sealed the deal with a kiss the crowd behind them erupted into cheers.

The End

BJ Wane

I live in the Midwest with my husband and our two dogs, a Poodle/Pyrenees mix and an Irish Water Spaniel. I love dogs, spending time with my daughter, babysitting her two dogs, reading and working puzzles. We have traveled extensively throughout the states, Canada and just once overseas, but I much prefer being a homebody. I worked for a while writing articles for a local magazine but soon found my interest in writing for myself peaking. My first book was strictly spanking erotica, but I slowly evolved to writing erotic romance with an emphasis on spanking. I love hearing from readers and can be reached here: bjwane@cox.net.

Recent accolades include: 5 star, Top Pick review from The Romance Reviews for *Blindsided*, 5 star review from Long & Short Reviews for Hannah & The Dom Next Door, which was also voted Erotic Romance of the Month on LASR, and my most recent title, Her Master At Last, took two spots on top 100 lists in BDSM erotica and Romantic erotica in less than a week!

Visit her Facebook page
https://www.facebook.com/bj.wane
Visit her website here
https://bjwaneauthor.com/

Don't miss these exciting titles by BJ Wane and Blushing Books!

Single Titles
Claiming Mia

Cowboy Doms Series
Submitting to the Rancher, Book 1
Submitting to the Sheriff, Book 2
Submitting to the Cowboy, Book 3
Submitting to the Lawyer, Book 4
Submitting to Two Doms, Book 5
Submitting to the Cattleman, Book 6
Submitting to the Doctor, Book 7

Virginia Bluebloods Series
Blindsided, Book 1
Bind Me To You, Book 2
Surrender To Me, Book 3
Blackmailed, Book 4
Bound By Two, Book 5
Determined to Master: Complete Series

Murder on Magnolia Island
Logan - Book 1
Hunter - Book 2
Ryder - Book 3
Murder on Magnolia Island: The Complete Series

Miami Masters
Bound and Saved - Book One
Master Me, Please - Book Two
Mastering Her Fear - Book Three
Bound to Submit - Book Four
His to Master and Own - Book Five
Theirs to Master - Book Six
Miami Masters Collection

Masters of the Castle
Witness Protection Program
(Controlling Carlie)

AudioBooks
Bound and Saved

Connect with BJ Wane
bjwane.blogspot.com

Blushing Books

Blushing Books is one of the oldest eBook publishers on the web. We've been running websites that publish spanking and BDSM related romance and erotica since 1999, and we have been selling eBooks since 2003. We hope you'll check out our hundreds of offerings at http://www.blushingbooks.com.

Blushing Books Newsletter

Please join the Blushing Books newsletter
to receive updates & special promotional offers.
You can also join by using your mobile phone:
Just text BLUSHING to 22828.

CPSIA information can be obtained
at www.ICGtesting.com
Printed in the USA
LVHW031829070720
660010LV00001B/89